LUSSI IN LOVE

A MONSTER BRIDES ROMANCE

ROSLYN ST. CLAIR

Cover Art: image by @ konradbak through Depositphoto.com

Background by Pexels from Pixabay through Bookbrush.com

Interior Art: shapes obtained through Bookbrush.com -design created by author

Edited by the fabulous Evil Commas

All characters and situations are solely the result of the author's imagination, and any crossover to this world and reality, or the people operating within it, is purely coincidental. Of course, as the old gods might tell you, there are no accidents, but only synchronicity. Any imagined connection might just be a sign directing you toward a greater truth: we are all archetypes, with more similarity than difference.

For more information, please contact author at Roslynstclair@yahoo.com

Additionally, for anyone interested, the story mentions Lucifer and Rose and Hell, more of which you can find in the Fated Archangels series. Trigger Warnings for Fated Archangels: DARK PNR with scenes of graphic sex and violence.

DEDICATED to all those friends, family, and boyfriends who tried to change me. Guess what? You failed; and

To Judy with Cats at Evil Commas- your editing, as always, is so perfect, I'm left in awe of your talent. I hope the characters are slightly more likable, and if so, that's because of you; and

To Monster Brides Monster Fans- you've become my home and family, the most perfect group of individuals ever to grace the book of Face; and

To S.C. Principale, who made Monster Brides possible and continues to let us/force us to live and thrive (in the gentlest way possible; and

To all Monster Lovers everywhere who find beauty and purpose in the most hideous of exteriors. And for all those who feel like a monster on the inside, I wish you love and light, with the hope you can learn to love what roars and growls within. This isn't an easy world. Sometimes, shoes pinch. We still must keep walking.

When an OCD(?) Lussi meets a guy who hasn't left a clean surface in his life...

A little history about Lussi, the Winter Witch of Norway, before we begin...

Normally, I like to include a little note about the mythological figures who take center stage in my novels to give readers an idea of the traditional guise worn by those who've demanded transformation and romance.

However, because my little historical note on mythology became too overwhelmingly long, I've moved it to the back of the novel. For those not interested (yet!) in the fascinating juxtaposition of Good versus Evil that Lussi represents, as well as the continued malignment of women, here's a brief blip on who Lussi is.

According to Norse legend, Lussi is either a witch, vette/vaettir (female spirit), or demon. On the night when December 12th turns into December 13th, the old Winter Solstice in the Julian calendar, Lussi rides with her horde of spirits, monsters (such as trolls), ghosts, or, (as is the case in this novel), demons. Together, they wreak destruction and death upon those caught outside, caught out of bed, or caught with chores unfulfilled or fulfilled in a slipshod manner.

Lussi and her horde are the terror of Norway, and though her day has been aligned in recent times with the probably Swedish import of St. Lucia, she remains a part of the majestic and often dangerous fjords and valleys that birthed her.

Lussi also kidnaps naughty children, and sometimes adults. The children simply disappear. The adults either disappear or are dropped elsewhere after having been roughed up a bit. Or a lot. (In this novel, Lussi kidnaps Nicholas Frye, and so their love story begins. She's also kidnapped children before the story begins, but only to keep them safe).

Lussi's legend pre-dates Christianity and was present during the Viking Age. No one is certain when she came into being, or how. (In this novel, she was born of a curse 1500 years ago).

Lussi is said to be pure evil. I think she wants to change, but getting rid of a bad reputation and disagreeable beginnings isn't easy. Luckily, she'll have some help...

CHAPTER ONE:

December 12-13 - *Lussi*

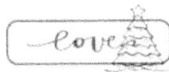

The clock screams at me, but I ignore it. Mostly.

Every year on the eve of the old Winter Solstice, just before the clock strikes midnight, I tell myself that I'm not going to speed off on some demented spree of malevolence and violence the minute the hour drops. Every year, I fly out the door, restraint left for someone else with more willpower.

But that's my problem: I can never help myself. Frankly, after fifteen hundred years of giving into my instincts, I'm a little sick of my lack of willpower. I'm tired.

Tonight, I want nothing more than to swig my diet cola, eat my herring on toast, maybe partake of a couple (or a few dozen) butter cookies the demon next door baked yesterday (and begrudgingly wrapped up for me when I just happened to walk by beneath his window as he removed them from the oven), and read a good book by the fire, but… the clock.

Six minutes. Six small minutes until midnight above shell.

Nope, not moving. I stare down at my reader and flip it to the next page before flipping it back. Something about a girl and a monster and…

Five minutes. I nibble on a cookie.

Sweat breaks out on my forehead as I force my throat to swallow. My eyes keep tracking to the damned second hand as it counts down the inevitable. It's too early to leave, but in one more minute, a single span of sixty small seconds, I'll be late on the only night in the entire above-shell year that matters to me. It's my night. *Lussi Langnatt.* I have responsibilities. Duties. Addictions to be placated.

Doesn't matter. No way am I leaving my home. I'm done with death and destruction, I'm done with kidnapping ill-cared-for children (because frankly, the orphanage is full, and I'm sick of their endless demands for candy and dangerous toys), and I'm most certainly done with knocking down chimneys. Last year, after toppling five, my hands were blistered for a full week.

No, I'm just going to sit here and sip the sweet bubbles of my diet cola. I used to drink regular cola. It made my breath smell like garlic. This artificial stuff, though... yum.

The ticking grows louder. It reverberates inside my bones.

Four minutes.

My door flies open. Sami, my personal assistant, rushes in all atwitter. "Oh, thank Hell you're still here. Marvin had a problem with the books, and one thing led to another, and..." He stutters to a stop. "Why aren't you dressed?"

I shrug. Not getting dressed.

Sami sighs. "We talked about this, Lussi. You can't wear pajamas. Someone will make fun of you, you'll kill them, and then you'll pout. No one likes a pouter, Winter Witch. And where are the others?"

He looks around the room before focusing on the hearth, as if a swarm of demons is going to projectile vomit from the flames.

I mean, they have in the past. It's not a completely unreasonable expectation, and I am supposed to be leading the horde on our annual pilgrimage of death and destruction tonight.

Nope. Not feeling it. Not going. Can't make me.

"Lussi? Where's the horde?"

"They showed up a half hour ago, drunk as usual, ready to ravage the world."

"And?" he presses when I don't say more. He looks around the room again, squinting in case some have gone invisible. Neat trick, sure, and certain demons can manage it, but there are no telltale ripples in the air.

"I sent them home."

He blinks. Five valuable seconds tick by. "Why?"

I shrug. "Not feeling it this year."

Sami blinks again and stares at me as if I've grown horns. I mean, I could grow them, I suppose. I am a self-actualizing monster, and if I wanted them, I'm sure I could pop a pair of glittery pink shells on top of my head, no problem.

Three minutes.

Ooh. Or lavender? I rather like the flowers because they smell delicious. I could grow a darling pair of petaled horns. Bonus? My demon horde can't stand the scent. And the soft purple color will go well with my clothing since I usually dress in white or gray.

Ooh, but what if I used some of Lucifer's copper to fashion a pair of Viking upside-down udders? The king's copper mine is only a day's brisk walk from my home, and since he's left Hell... could I dare sneak in? I could magick the metal, but there's something satisfying about constructing with one's hands.

And now I'm fixated on horns. I check the top of my head for telltale bumps in case I've begun to self-actualize without knowing it, but my hair still falls flat.

Anyway, I'd probably just obsess over them, and I have enough obsessions without adding to my list. Plus, why fool with what works? Femme fatale today is almost always tomorrow's, "What the Hell was I thinking?" Just look at the '80s.

"Stop feeling your head!" Sami bangs his fist into his forehead.

That's got to hurt. He has razor-like projections surrounding his face when he's above shell. Sometimes, he self-actualizes them below shell as well. He's great in a bar fight, or so he tells me, but his wince, along with the green blood dripping down his arm, says he probably should have engaged in a little double-think before acting out his frustration.

I'm almost ready to tell him so when the clock finishes another circuit.

Two minutes. The time swirls in my blood.

"What in the name of Holy Hell is wrong with you?" Sami waves his hand in front of my face. "You're The Winter Witch! Lussi of the Long Night. You are the leader of the Horde, the terror of Norway, the bane of the civilized world, and more feared than Krampus, Hans Trapp, Belsnickel, and the Jólakötturinn combined! You can't 'not feel it,' Lussi."

"And yet, here we are." I wave my hand as my heart beats with the ticking clock.

"I don't understand."

"What's to understand? Can't a witch change her mind?"

One minute and ten seconds.

Sami's gaze locks on the moving hand. He begins to tremble. "Please, Lussi. You've got commitments. A purpose. And the horde. Do you have any idea what mischief they'll wreak if you don't control them tonight? The veil between the worlds is so thin, there's no way some demons won't escape even if you order all of us contained. And the results will be your fault."

Left unsaid is the rest: my fault and my guilt. I don't do well with guilt which I've only recently begun to feel the past couple years. It's a horrible emotion. Like cats clawing each other in a bag, only the bag is my chest.

Thirty seconds.

Fine. I sigh and flip the velvet blanket from my lap as I stand. Sami rushes and catches it before the wrinkles can distract me. With his other hand, he pushes me towards the portal circle, where the veil is the thinnest between the worlds. On December 13th, the old winter equinox in the Julian calendar, above shell and below shell collide, so I don't even need to use magick to see between the realms. The upper world lies like a snowy portrait I can just walk into.

"You'll fold the blanket? The way I like?"

"And center it on the chair, yes, yes. I'll bring the horde. Give me five minutes to round them up and send them after you, but for Hell's sake, just go! No—wait!" He gestures at my footie pajamas imprinted with gray cats.

"Right." With a twist of my wrist, I change into a filmy dress, just perfect for setting the world straight. It's gray, so it probably won't show the dirt.

I take another second to look through the portal. In theory, I could be late. The veil will remain thin all night. But in practice, being late is one of those sins I find impossible to commit. Late is every bit as wrong as squeezing toothpaste from the top of the tube.

"Go!" Sami shouts.

Fine. But only because I'm suddenly wondering about the Jorgenson farm. It's just up over the hill. With eight children under the age of twelve, there's always a bit of chaos to punish, although after I stole little Torben from his crib last year, I'm hoping the family has learned its lesson and I'll be able to return him. That's always the goal. So few, though, manage.

And there are those clawing cats again, set upon my insides for reasons I can't fathom.

Rubbing my chest, I step into the icy landscape just as the clock sounds the hour. The fjords visible to my left are so lovely that my spirit instantly lifts, and the cats subside.

I try so hard to make everything perfect around me, and yet the earth is so beautiful in the symmetry of its dissymmetry, I often wonder why I bother trying to make matters right.

For several moments, I don't move. The air above shell is so much fresher than below. The colors are more vibrant, even at night. Even in winter.

Finally, taking a deep breath of the chill air, I lift from the ground and speed through the air. My demons will find me. Not only are they bound to me while I walk above shell, we've done this dance fifteen hundred times before. They know my route, as unchanging as, well, me.

Maybe I should grow horns. Complacency is a gateway sin.

CHAPTER TWO:

Lussi

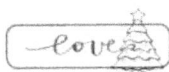

I drop down over the hill onto the Jorgenson farm and feel a little lift in my spirit. Not a single fence post sways out of alignment. The stairs are swept. The land under the white snow and bright stars twinkles without a litter of stray branches. The house has been painted a new shade of red. The chimney has been rebricked. I'm so delighted, I almost don't want to look within.

But I have to. It's my sacred obligation.

Okay. Maybe not so much obligation as a need to know that everything is in order.

My heart thumps when I spot the mother snoring on the rickety couch. In her lap, she holds a book. The book isn't even. It lists to one side. So does she.

I try to turn away. I do. I have a long night in front of me, and I know in my heart the woman's sins are not so grievous they deserve punishment this year, especially as I deprived her of her baby just last year, but... she's out of bed. That's a no-no. Plus, the book.

With a sigh, I slip down the chimney and cross to Mrs. Jorgenson. Wrapping my arms over my chest, I tap my foot as I stare daggers at her and wait for her to wake. I mean, I don't have all night. I clear my throat, but the exhausted woman doesn't react.

Fine. Pulling back my leg, I kick her square in the shin.

Mrs. Jorgenson jumps awake, the book falling from her hands and spreading along the floor.

Worse and worse. Anger, bright and red, begins rushing through me.

"What the... oh!" Her eyes widen as she recognizes me. She scrambles back and away, over the arm, falling flat on her generous behind, making more disorder with each passing second.

I glance back at the book and frown.

She must feel my ire because she begins babbling. "Lussi! I-I'm sorry. I fell asleep. But I cleaned and made sure everything was straightened, and... look."

She dives for the book, trembling so hard she nearly drops it. When she has it in her hands, she snaps it closed before spinning for the bookshelf. There, in an open spot, she tucks in the novel, carefully aligning the edge so that no single book creeps out past the others.

I so appreciate the care she takes that I decide not to punish her for her infraction. "Next year," I say, pointing my finger, "I won't be so nice."

I begin to walk back to the hearth when she stops me. "Wait!"

When I turn, she's wringing her hands together. "My Torben. Is he...?"

Torben. The tow-headed boy of two years. He has a sweet tooth and a love of horse figures. A sudden pang and squall of fighting cats in my chest makes me want to flee, but I force myself to speak first. "He's fine. Doing well, actually. He loves horses and candy." My gaze drifts around the pristine room. The family has come so far in the past year. "If you maintain the farm as you've been doing, I'll consider sending him back to you. You've remembered to feed the others supper?"

"Yes! Yes, Lussi. Every night." She bobs her head, seeking to reassure me.

"Fine. But I'll be watching." Yet, there are those cats again, scraping long claws down my veins.

Her great, watery blue eyes blink before she throws herself at my feet. "Thank you, thank you, Lussi! Thank you!"

Eww.

Without another word, I speed up the chimney and back into the air, but the uneasy feeling follows me as I pass over the Fjaerland district. The stunning vistas move my soul as nowhere else ever has. The area surrounding Fjaerlandsfjord, a branch of the Sognefjord, is almost desolate. Peaceful. Lush in the absence of bustling humans; it has a clawlike beauty.

Three kilometers from the main road, the town of Mundal provides tourists with an opportunity to walk where humans have made their habitation since the Stone Age. The views are killer, but the comfiness is what draws me. The town is a light in the darkness, bracketed as it is by barren, virile, perilous nature. The twinkling Yule lights and fir branches make it festive.

If ever I am forced to live above shell, I will make this town my home. I could run an inn and serve *fårikål*, the national dish of mutton and cabbage flavored with whole black peppercorns and salt. I'd plate *eplekake*, my favorite apple cake, for dessert with a nice glass of sugared tea.

I shake away the pipe dream and fly faster.

When I set down, thirty of my most avid demons appear beside me. Tethered to me by an energetic rope, they stay close unless I let them wander, which I often do. Norway is large. Plus, no one wants to be yanked back like a dog. It's humiliating, even for a demon.

"The farmers first?" Rotten asks, baring his yellow fangs. He rubs his palms together with glee. "Or the tourists?"

"Tourists last, I suppose. Farmers first. Others in the middle."

There's so much disorder in humanity, it sets my teeth on edge, but I have levels of ire and need. Tourists live from suitcases and emptied plastic bottles, their sundries strewn around in casual chaos, but the farmers who don't plow their entire fields? Who've left piles of rot at the edges of their properties or allowed their fences to sag?

Jul is a sacred time and has been since before I was created. To enter the sacred season without first putting life to rights is unacceptable. It's an intolerable insult. The very idea of such sloth fills me with a rage so strong, it's a wonder I can see past the red mist.

Fortunately, or unfortunately, depending upon one's point of view, only twenty farms remain viable in the district. This age has loosened the grasp of the land. Now, most of the three hundred or so residents live in the town and suburbs, or if they live where the snow stretches, they do things like write or tap upon computers.

My horde cackles with wild glee as I lead them over fields. Too soon, I spy a sheep pen with a trough tilted off-axis. Is it evilness enough to punish? Inside the small farm with its flock of twenty-two lives a mother, a father, and a small tow-haired boy with green eyes, aged five and three-quarters. They sleep soundly, the boy dreaming of running along the stream with his dog, Vali.

"Here, Lady?" Sami demands. "Here?"

I should give the order, but I can't. The rest of the residence is pristine, with all the edges squared, all the corners dusted. A glittering tree stands in the corner. More branches spread the scent of pine. No candles remain lit, threatening fire. There's love in this home, and for a moment, my chest pangs. Not clawing cats this time, but something I can't place, something sugary and weepy.

I rub at the strange sensation, but it doesn't dissipate.

Odd. But the tilted trough must bother me more than I'd thought.

"Not here. Spread out, keep to the rules, and report back." I loosen the cords and allow my horde flight while I drop below. The trough is rusted at the edges. Old. Worn. I hate the signs of decay with a white-hot passion, and I need to... well, I shouldn't. It's not my role.

Glancing around, hoping to appear casual should anyone see me since I've got a reputation to maintain, I touch my finger to the feed pen and gather my will. A flare of magick sparkles from the tip. Instantly, the trough straightens and renews.

Relief flares through me. I feel better. Lighter.

At the next farm, though, matters cannot be similarly rectified. One human sits in his bed, reading with one of those battery-powered book lights. The pages of the book are folded. The spine has gotten wet, so it warps like a wilting blossom.

Even worse, the house is a pigsty that not even the filthiest hog would deign to call home. Cans and dirty dishes line the kitchen counters. Clothing is strewn around the bedroom. No animals live within the boundary except small mice, rats, and other vermin, but they're chattering up a storm, telling me all about the grievous sins committed within the property. Additionally, fields have been left in disarray, the crops withered and bent at odd angles from the snow.

And I am filled with rage again. Rage at the abuse. Rage at the waste.

Rage at the odd angles and disarray.

Filling my chest with an icy bite of air, I flick my fingers and send out my magick. I cannot kill the human who is, technically, abed, but I can stomp on his chimney. I can cave in his walls. I can send my demons to torment him with their mischief.

Five of my horde swarm, sensing my ire. The human, trapped, opens his mouth in confusion as the roof tumbles around him. He looks up to see my demons dancing along the edge of the broken tiles. They set up whirlwinds and overturn whatever small order might originally have been present within the chaos.

I nod with satisfaction, but strangely, the knowledge I've fulfilled my duty doesn't sit well. I want to...

I want to clean up the mess, both what the human made and what I've created in trying to straighten the impossibly chaotic homestead.

As always, cleaning up the entire country is impossible. Why are these humans so stupid?

A scream of frustration wells in my throat. I cannot bite it back.

CHAPTER THREE:

Nicholas Frye

The words won't come. Every time I chase them, they retreat. Maybe it's because my ideas are too farfetched to stick to the page. Maybe it's fear of expressing them, which makes sense as they're batshit crazy.

I type a sentence, check my notes, and erase what I've just written. My evidence wouldn't convince a child of five.

Throwing back my head, I close my eyes. I'm going to be the laughingstock of the conference. I should never have agreed to give a speech on *Supernatural Psychosis: The Underpinnings of Augmented Reality in the Twenty-first Century.* The topic is so controversial it sounds like someone should be twisting their finger against the side of their head while shouting, "Cuckoo, cuckoo," when talking about me.

I'm not crazy, or if I am, there's a whole lot of people in the world waking up insane of late. As society crumbles at the hands of shysters and worse, more and more of my patients believe they're seeing behind the veil.

Some see ghosts. Others see demons or monsters. One is sure her car wants to have sex with her. The uptick in sightings of anthropomorphic and cryptozoological beings keeps increasing. No fewer than sixty-seven of my seventy-three current patients report interaction with the supernatural.

Their numbers and collective experiences suggest something unnatural is slithering up from the shadows. Lives are being ruined because of it. People's suffering needs to be addressed. But lecturing the world's most preeminent psychologists on the possibility of truth behind the massive wave of similar psychoses?

I'd rather battle demons.

My colleagues believe patients want us to cure them of delusions. Instead, I'm afraid mine are converting me to their fantasies.

Not the woman who's having sex with her car, of course. I refuse to believe that an inanimate thing can become sentient and self-serving. But for many of the others

I treat, it's getting harder and harder to convince myself that they're all just suffering DSM-5 disorders. Something is happening outside Science, with a capital "S".

It could be mass formation psychosis, but if so, what's the origin? The catapult? And why? Why now?

The outer fringe believes shadow governments are spraying us with chemicals, poisoning us with 5G, and inserting nano-tech into our bodies. Given the craziness in the world, anything is possible, but if that's the underpinning of the slew of supernatural reports, it's outside my purview.

Then again, so is the supernatural as a whole.

Enhancing evolution, maybe? Are we experiencing a pole shift on the cellular level?

I slip my gaze away from the computer screen, only to stare blankly at the wall. I can think of a number of explanations, none of them without problems. A sigh escapes me as I run my hands over my face. Exhaustion has left creases I can feel with my fingers.

I have to find a cause that doesn't make me sound batshit in front of five hundred of my colleagues or the *IAPR, The International Association of Psychological Researchers,* is going to kick me to the curb. Theories without evidence, a roadmap without actual signposts—these won't convince professionals who follow canonical Science with the zealotry of ardent priests.

No, I'll need hardcore proof if I want to convince my colleagues to investigate with me. Critical thinking in our profession long ago devolved into a rigid band of acceptable questions and answers. Psychologists possess a choice between clinging to mainstream academic consensus, or dishonor. Few will jump at the chance to embrace mockery on the basis of the flimsy supposition and logic I'm offering.

And what I'm suggesting demands critical thought. What I wouldn't give for some hard evidence.

Shoving aside the take-out box of what purports to be American pizza (and isn't, not by a long shot), I take a swig of whiskey. It's surprisingly good. The underbody catches in my throat and warms me from within. A small shiver of delight traces over my skin. Warm is good. Norway is cold. The freeze hasn't left my limbs since I stepped off the plane in Oslo.

I'm about to erase another line of text when the temperature in the room suddenly plummets. The air begins to swirl. A whirl of wind forms in the middle of the floor.

What the...?

I spin my chair to face whatever is happening when frigid fingers trail up my spine. I check the clock across the room and glance towards my briefcase. I should have pulled out the book on Norwegian myths before settling in earlier.

Because damn me for a fool. It's 12:52 a.m. on December 13th. Not a person in Norway fails to dread this night, though I can't remember if the pages I'd skimmed on the plane listed a way to foil the monster to whom this span of hours belongs.

Even as my blood ices and my heart begins racing with panic, the rest of me stutters to a stall. Even if I could run, I'm too late.

The myth steps out of thin air, catching me unprepared. A quick glance around the room reveals what I already know: I've left the space looking like a cyclone just swept through. Disorder? It's chaos.

My pulse kicks up, my bladder seizes, and my bones freeze, but a part of me I can't deny jumps with excitement. I wanted proof? Well, here she is, my very own supernatural experience.

Also, my death sentence. Lussi of the Long Night, The Winter Witch of Norway. My mother was right. I should have cleaned my room and been more careful what I wished for.

But when The Winter Witch locks gazes with me, she is nothing like what I imagined when I read her tale in my book. She's not hideous. No, she's strangely... magnificent.

Tall and thin, she wears a pale gray gossamer gown that leaves her arms bare, as if the ridiculous climate is as warm as a summer day on the equator. She's shapely and naked beneath the thin layers, giving me a glimpse of pink nipples and a shadowed vee between her legs.

I'm a man. Even seconds from my death, I'm going to focus on a female's anatomy.

I trail my gaze down and back up to the most perfect face I've ever seen. Topped with an array of wild, silver-white hair, she has a small chin, full pink lips, high cheekbones, and enormous gray eyes... but her nose is hooked just enough to ruin the perfection, and strangely, it makes her all the more perfect.

"Stunning." The whisper leaves my lips without my permission, but she's... "Perfect."

Her frown deepens.

But the most disorienting aspect of her face is the third eye sitting smack in the middle of her wide forehead. Also gray, it stares at me without blinking, catching my bones and crushing them beneath her disdain.

"Sorry. You're just... wow." Before I can drag more defeat out of the jaws of... er, defeat... I reach for my heavy crystal rocks glass with a blind, shaking hand. The crystal bangs into my teeth when I try to down my whisky. To cover my nerves, I ask, "Can I offer you a drink? Er, Lussi, is it?"

All three of her eyes briefly widen before her shapely lips tilt downward into a sneer.

Good thing I'm sitting. I'd quaver into a heap of jelly otherwise. "No? That's fine. But if you don't mind, I need the fortification." I chug the contents before I wipe the back of my hand across my lips.

In response, Lussi's hooked nose wrinkles with disgust.

The Winter Witch of Norway is in my room. My messy room. And for some reason, my testosterone-laden body is aroused, even as I'm terrified out of my gourd.

I'm not sure what to do. Should I start a conversation? Does she speak English? I don't speak Norwegian other than the smattering of words I've learned with which to order dinner. I'm fairly certain the gorgeous, ravaging supernatural force won't want to discuss menu items with a mortal she's come to kill.

She steps right through the furnishings as if they don't exist, as if her corporeal form is so insubstantial, she might as well be a ghost. None of her eyes leave me as she approaches without the least hesitation. Distaste is written in her every movement as she grabs her skirts to avoid my used workout clothing piled next to my bed.

Finally, she stands in front of me, as solid as I am. Looking down, she ignores the way I spread my knees so she can come closer (like I said—I'm a man. I'm a man, and she's... hot in an icy way that gets my blood pumping exactly where it shouldn't).

"Nicholas Frye. You debase the world. You take order and create chaos. I hereby find you guilty of..."

She knows my name. Of course, she does. She's magick.

"Of finding you amazing," I interrupt before she can finish passing sentence upon me in my language, thus answering one of my questions. "I know why you're here, but..." I shake my head and offer her a rickety smile. "You're incredible. Are you sure I can't offer you a drink? The other glass is clean." I jiggle the one I'm still clutching between my shaking fingers.

Not bad, Nick. You've just survived five seconds with Lussi without dying. It might be a record.

Moments tick by before she answers. "The delay of a shared drink will not save you, Nicholas Frye."

"Who says I need saving?"

Despite my inner mortal terror, I push off from the arms of the desk chair and stand. I'm taller, but I'm so close to Lussi I can see the amazing porcelain quality of her skin. Not a line or a pockmark mars her flesh. Even her nose, up close, is a thing of beauty. Hooked, yes, but if one didn't have an idea of what a nose should look like, hers would be the masterpiece used to define the body part.

"I do. Because I must destroy you now," she explains, the accented English bubbling like a brook from her lips. I can imagine her singing those ancient Norwegian heart-wrenching songs, all fury, despair, and longing for love.

Despite the fullness of her vocalizations, a death sentence is still a death sentence. Still, her forehead wrinkles around her third eye, as if she might not really wish to kill me.

Many a man has had less to work with, and I'm up for the challenge. Literally.

I lean towards her, drawn more by the way her cool flesh boils my blood than by any attempt to save my life, though I suppose the one doesn't negate the other. And maybe the way her cheeks pinken in a slight blush means I'm not alone in noticing the bed behind her.

On the other hand, she's studying me like I'm a bug under glass. She's all disdain and disgust, but for those little dots of color on her skin.

I wink and reach around her for the bottle of whiskey, intentionally invading her personal space. "Maybe we could reach Heaven together."

A look of shock rounds her mouth and eyes before her lips twitch into a tiny, seemingly reluctant smile. "Did you just try to seduce me with a lame line?"

"Yup. Did it work?"

"No." But her lashes fall—so maybe, yes?

And of course, my dick hardens further.

The alcohol I pour sloshes into the glass. I offer it to her, and our fingers meet at the exchange. Hers are ice in need of warming, so I leave mine beneath hers, offering my heat. Offering me.

There's nothing like a dangerous woman to get my blood pumping. I've tried to settle for reasonable women, but they're boring. Uncomplicated. I'm a man driven to extremes by fascination and mystery, ergo my profession, which allows me to explore within. It's also why I'm still single. I need the adrenalin rush.

The one I'm feeling now is enough to propel me up a mountain.

As a reasonably attractive, unattached male in possession of a PhD and a healthy bank account, and as someone who's always loved the chase and the dance even more than the inevitable entanglement of bodies, I've had a lot of dates. I've never felt this level of hunger right from the start. It's so overwhelming, my entire body is wound up like I'm at the finish line rather than on the starting block.

Given the tightness of my jeans, the swell is painful. I shift in the hopes of moving my unruly member into a more comfortable position without her noticing.

Her glance drops, and she smirks.

"I suppose you're used to men overreacting when you're around."

"Usually, they're on the floor begging and promising me the world if I don't slay them."

"Show off."

The look she sends me doesn't promise death. There's a hint of laughter in her eyes, a hint of the same hunger I'm feeling.

Yup. I can work with that.

CHAPTER FOUR:

Nick

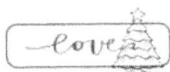

Lussi quirks a brow at me before stepping back and breaking our contact. I release the glass to her. After a long sniff, she delicately places her lips to the edge and takes a small sip. I know the minute she senses the fire because all her eyes grow wide and her lips open, revealing a pink tongue to match the nipples beading under her gossamer gown.

So, she does feel it, too, whatever weird chemistry exists between us.

Because whiskey alone doesn't pebble a nipple. Thoughts of the heat of a man's mouth might. I hope.

"What in all of Hell is this?" Just as I'd done earlier, she begins to wipe her lips with the back of her hand, stops, and frowns before wrapping her fingers back around the glass.

"Whiskey. Haven't you ever tried it?" I don't wait for an answer as her tongue snakes over her lips, wiping away the residual ghost of liquid. I use my foot to pull out the stationary chair adjacent to me at the round table where I've been working. "Please. Sit."

For a moment, she hesitates. My breath catches as she glances around the room once more, but releases when she sinks into the seat like a flow of water, her bones operating without the usual creaks, groans, and hard edges that herald human movement.

I'm sitting with a monster. I don't know what to say, what to ask first, and I don't want to disrupt the delicate balance of possibility I'm trying to build between us. She's skittish, like one of my patients, all fawn-like tension, ready to flee if she senses danger, except she's the peril. But I've had patients like that before, too.

Falling back on my professional training, I say, "So, tell me about yourself, Lussi. May I call you, Lussi?" At her nod, I continue. "I confess, you fascinate me."

"I do?" Her head tilts to the side as she studies me.

I nod. "I've just been reading about you, but to find you in the flesh..." I let my eyes heat on the last word, and I'm gratified by the blush that again brushes her cheeks. "Can I ask you about yourself? Maybe about your life, or your dreams?"

Her head tilts the other way. "Dreams?"

"Dreams. What you wish for out of life." I shift in my chair as I force myself into a thin semblance of professionalism. "What makes you tick, Lussi?"

A slight frown pulls at her full lips. "I don't have dreams. I don't tick. I am The Winter Witch of Norway. I have responsibilities."

"Like?"

"Like keeping order in a world constantly running to entropy, ruin, and chaos. I have a duty to punish people like you, Nicholas Frye." She pauses. "You might say I get off on it."

"Ooh. Very nice." A purr rumbles through me at the flirtatious double entendre. "I wholeheartedly approve of what you just did there."

"Lovely. I was worried."

A small laugh at her sarcastic retort escapes me. She truly is magnificent. "You should know—turnabout is always okay with me. I like a woman on top, though I have a tendency to take control." I pause before adding, "But I'd make sure you enjoyed every position."

My pants are far too tight. She's far too sexy in the most terrifying of ways.

"I'm always on top, Nicholas Frye, and I always enjoy every position, most particularly because I decide them." She winks with her third eye, and I groan.

Fuck. I'm a sucker for playful banter.

But her frown returns when she gestures about the room. "You should be ashamed. You're a disaster walking on two legs."

True. My suitcase is lying open, still half-packed. Clothing lies strewn about the room, random socks and underwear peppering the pieces of furniture and floor. Toiletries, old food boxes from the past few days, bottles, and papers litter the space. For three days, I've lived out of this room while trying to find the perfect words for the presentation. And with every elusive syllable, another mess has been created.

"Right. It's a little messy, sure. I've been working on a deadline with a theory I can't support and..."

"You've created disorder from the order you were given." She leans forward, iced fire sparking in her gray eyes.

She's not wrong. "Messiness is a failing I own. And what about you, Lussi? What are your failings?"

When in doubt, turn tables. Talk to her like a therapist to a patient... like a good therapist with a patient that he's not attracted to.

Which also means I should cut out the flirtation and sexual banter, which is a shame. I adore these first moments with a desirable woman. Too bad they never last longer than the sex that follows. I keep hoping the attraction will morph into deeper feeling, though so far, it hasn't.

One day.

I push the thought away, but it doesn't go far. There's something about Lussi, all simmering frigid heat waiting to boil over. The thrill of danger. There's something about her that feels like the destination rather than the road.

Probably, the destination is my death. I should have made my bed. Maybe then, she'd join me in it.

She narrows her gray eyes upon me, caging the storms I sense rising within her. "Order is everything I am, Nicholas Frye."

"That's clearly not true."

She raises a brow.

"Besides, messiness shouldn't be a mortal sin."

"Perhaps not to you, but you will unfortunately soon find that it is to me." With a swish of gauze, she places her glass neatly on the drinks tray, and while she does, she lines up the bottle, too. Eyeing my glass, she frowns.

Fascinating how the little things can distract her. I lean toward her. "What are you thinking?"

With a twist of her fingers, she uses magick to steal my glass away. In the next instant, two sparkling glasses and one bottle line up in the center of the tray.

"I'm thinking I need to organize your room."

"I'm not done with my drink."

"You are." She stares at me with intent.

"I'm not."

She looks away first. She checks the tray and bites her bottom lip.

So, she likes a firm hand, my Lussi.

Seriously. At this rate, I'm going to go at her like a fifteen-year-old teen with his first girlie magazine.

Fortunately for the state of my restraint, she rises and begins cleaning up the disaster of a room. As she does, a tiny trickle of hope bubbles up inside me. I recognize her. She's like quite a few of my patients who suffer from various forms and levels of OCD.

She turns to glare at my disorganized suitcase, unaware she's just offered me a glimpse into her psyche. "How can you live like this?"

I shrug. "It works for me. Why? What would you do differently?"

She immediately takes the bait. "Obviously, your undergarments should be folded and arranged by intended wearing date from front to back in the top drawer. In half, and then in thirds."

"That's a lot of math."

Rolling all three of her eyes at me, she demonstrates with the pair of boxers I've left hanging half in and half out of my suitcase. "Like this." She holds up a neat package before slipping it into the top drawer, but then frowns again as it begins to unravel.

With a wave of her fingers, she stops the problem. Defying gravity and all kinds of physics, the folded garment remains together as if held with glue.

She looks at me and smiles until I point out, "But I don't have magick at my disposal. What would you do without it?" But when she only frowns at the boxers, I add, "You see? Being organized isn't as easy for a human as it is for a Winter Witch."

"Others manage, Nicholas Frye. Books have been written on the subject. By humans." While she speaks, she begins picking up other items. Socks. More boxers. Pants. Shirts. Some, she folds. Others, she takes to the closet, and when she discovers an insufficient number of hangers, she waves her hand and creates more.

I grab my glass and fill it with more whiskey before I sink back into my chair to watch and sip as Lussi makes short work of my pile of clothing. The items remaining on the floor, she scoops up and dumps into the trash can.

"Hey, I need those." I stand up and reach for the rectangular metal bin, but she resists and clutches it to her chest.

"They're dirty."

"Right. I can wash everything and wear them again. Plus, I'm fond of that sweater." I pause. If Lussi were really my patient, I wouldn't offer any insights into my life. But she's not. Yet.

She shouldn't ever be, not with how I'm reacting to her.

Though, treating her for her obvious disorder would be a professional coup, and a way to study her magick.

I push the selfish thoughts aside. "My mother gave the sweater to me for my last birthday. She didn't knit it herself, but she sewed my name onto the tag like she used to do when I was young. Said she missed me being a little boy."

For a moment, Lussi looks confused, before a soft pink blush stains her cheeks. "You have a mother?"

"I do. I'm very fond of her."

Sexual interest/potential girlfriend or patient? How do I treat The Winter Witch? Because taking her as a patient could also save me from her wrath and have a welcome byproduct of actually helping her.

Taking her to bed—that could save me too, unless she's a black widow. But releasing some sexual tension won't ultimately aid her for more than a few hours. It won't free the delicate supernatural entity from living a life crippled by an obsessive-compulsive disorder.

"What's she like?" The small question catches me with its forlorn quality.

And my dick tells my brain and conscience to shut up. A vulnerable, dangerous, supernatural beauty who responds to a firm hand? All my protective instincts rise up and join the desire swirling within me. Add to the mix the adrenalin surge at the potential peril, and potential girlfriend it is.

"My mother? She's lovely. Accepting. She had me late in life, after thinking she was barren. She, my father, and I had five wonderful years together before he was killed. He was an accountant. You would have approved of his neat and orderly lines of figures."

Lussi sinks onto the bed. I think she's forgotten about the mess and the trashcan she holds because she's so focused upon my face, I feel her settle upon me like mist. "How was he taken from you, Nicholas Frye? And did you love him, too?"

I sink back down, my hands folding around the glass I hold between my spread knees. The inevitable heartache fills me as I think about my father. I don't often tell my story, but why not to her? She may well be my end. She should know who she's executing.

"I adored him, though he had ties to the Irish freedom fighters. One day, the head of the local organization showed up on our doorstep with an envelope full of cash, his sincere condolences, and a suggestion we not ask too many questions."

"And did you? Ask questions?"

"No. I was a child, and later, I didn't want to endanger my mother."

"Whom you love."

"Yes."

She tilts her head to the other side, but I can't unravel what she's thinking. Does she hate me because of my blood connection to the unscrupulous? Or does she pity me because I lost my parent so young?

At least she's not making any move to kill me. Plus, she's tidied my room quite nicely, but since I started talking about my parents, she's allowed a lone sock and tee-shirt to lie on the floor.

OCD, but maybe not so severe she can't be cured. Maybe not OCD at all, actually, but as a working hypothesis, the categorization is a place to start. Or end.

Stupid brain. It's a lot easier when my dick is in charge.

"Why are you staring at me like you're unpeeling an orange and wish to examine me for pips?" Her softly Norwegian-accented words don't sound upset so much as intrigued.

Shuffling my feet a little wider, I clear my throat. Is it bravery or stupidity coursing through me? But I'm curious. I'm always curious, and she's the most mysterious being I've ever met. She's a magical creature. Of course I want to unravel her down to her frigid bones, even if she ultimately kills me for the pleasure.

But what a presentation I could provide if she doesn't hack me to pieces.

"I want to help you, Lussi."

"Help me?" Her eyes narrow. "I don't need help."

"Don't you?" I wave at the trashcan she holds. "I can heal you."

Her lips purse against a smile. "What presumption. It's not an illness that will make me take your life, Nicholas Frye. It is purpose."

She begins to stand. This is the tricky part. It is with every patient who comes to me because someone else made them. This time, my life is on the line.

Swirling the whiskey in my glass, I nod. "What you call purpose, Lussi, is likely a very treatable obsessive-compulsive disorder, though I'd have to administer some tests to be certain."

"Oh, how I love modern terms." But she sinks back. "You think I'm disordered because I'm going to kill you?"

"The threat is part of it, as is the fact you mentioned you feel a duty to create order from chaos. You also mentioned not understanding what it is to dream, which makes me sad for you."

Bad therapist. I shouldn't express emotions, especially to a reluctant patient. Therapy isn't about me.

My dick shrinks a little, aware we've decided on patient, not date.

What I can see of Lussi's chest above the rim of the waste can rises with breath and falls as her eyes glitter. She makes no sound. I've managed to strike a blow I didn't intend.

"Haven't you ever wondered what your life might be like if you weren't subject to the restrictions of order and duty?"

"My purpose is not a disorder, and you're not half as bright as you think you are." Her clipped tone denudes her softly accented voice of its kindness.

Minefields everywhere, and not a solid place to step. I clear my throat. "I want to help."

All traces of humor disappear. Rage hardens her features. Her fingers clench on the metal bucket.

She's going to kill me.

I clear my throat. "I'm a psychologist. Not to brag, but I'm well-known and respected in my field." And sometimes mocked, especially recently when I ask colleagues about their experiences with the supernatural. I'll leave that part out of my bio. "I've helped a lot of people deal with various anxieties, such as how to confront chaos and the fear it brings." I pause and let the last word sink in, hoping it hits her where it counts. "And if you would allow me to assist you, I believe I could offer you a new lease on life."

"How gallant of you." Danger hisses around her syllables.

I swallow and press on. "Not gallant. Committed to helping those who suffer unnecessarily."

"I assure you, my suffering is most necessary. As will be yours." She raises her fingers, but just as I expect to be struck down or set on fire, she pauses. Her hand wraps around the bin again. "Though it isn't pleasant, my existence." Her low-voiced admission seems wrangled from her very soul.

A smattering of hope fills me again. "It must be terrible, Lussi. I can't imagine how you suffer—but you could tell me." I lean towards her. "I can't truly guarantee a cure, I suppose, but I can promise that you'll feel better just for talking about your feelings. I'm a very good listener, and I won't judge."

Her back straightens. Anger flashes in her eyes. "No one judges me, Nicholas Frye, and lives."

"I can help you discount the messes of the world," I continue, doing my best to ignore the threat. "I can help ease the loneliness of your self-induced isolation."

The last is a stab in the dark born of experience with other perfectionists. When the world fails to match a perfectionist's idea of how it should be, he or she often avoids it rather than risking further disappointment.

But as Lussi leans forward, my death is in her eyes. She raises her hand once more. I shut my eyes tight, my lips firming as I wince and wait for the blow.

My mother, who always says I talk too much, is right again.

CHAPTER FIVE:

Lussi

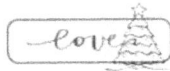

I know Nicholas Frye believes I mean to strike him dead. In truth, I'm not certain why I hesitate. The mussy-haired bastion of disorder certainly deserves to be punished. I've dealt the blow before to those who've merely laid a pen out of alignment. Because it's my job. It's my calling. It is who I am. Long before Lucifer had a change of heart and confined my nature to only one country on a single night of the year, parameters that pinch just as much as a new pair of shoes, I existed to right the world.

But instead of killing Nicholas, I drop my hand back to the trashcan and place the pail on the floor. Rising, I move slowly toward the human I can't seem to kill. I wait until his eyes open before I stroke the edge of his square jaw.

Prickly stubble stings the pads of my fingers. I should hate it. Stubble is disorder. But something inside me tightens. The feeling isn't pleasant, but it's like eating candy: once I start, I don't want to stop, not even when my stomach revolts.

Desire. Something I shouldn't feel for this catastrophic human being. I have needs, and I take care of them, but this cramping inside me? This yearning to press my lips against his and test their strength and softness? That's new.

Scalded, I draw my fingers back. "You have no understanding of my nature, human. What you suggest is insulting and ridiculous."

"Is it? I never meant it to be."

Even his eyes reflect disorder, a chaos of brown, green, and gold. Why they hold my attention and bait my breath, I don't know. Maybe because they're like twin masterpieces, imbued with swirls of colors and designs that should prove inharmonious but aren't. Like nature itself, they balance in their imperfection.

"What did you mean?"

"To help you, Lussi, that's all. To ease the pain I see in you."

Help me. Fix me. Save himself. All those reasons swirl in his incredible eyes. I don't sense deception so much as incompleteness in his response.

A flash of anger rushes through me. I despise half-truths as much as full-out lies. I raise my hand again, but I can't summon my deadly magick even though I know I should slay this infuriating mortal and continue on with my night.

My demons flurry around Norway. While conversing, I've allowed their leash to extend too far. With a twist of my wrist, I draw them back tighter—but not into the room, not yet. I keep them on guard around the building, knowing they hate me for my power and their imprisonment to my will.

Not that I care. They're demons. No one cares what demons think.

"I'm not in pain," I deny, keeping my voice soft.

When I fail to terminate him, Nicholas's shoulders sag with relief. "What would you call what you're feeling?"

"Enraged. You know what I am, mortal, but not *who* I am. Your temerity in thinking..."

Unbelievably, he grabs my hand in his and draws the back of it to his lips. The brush against my skin is fire. Uncomfortable sparks flicker up my arm.

Jerking back, he releases my hand. A flush of red skims over his lightly tanned skin as he realizes what he's done. "I'm sorry. I..." His gaze flits away before returning. "I'm a therapist. I know better than to touch a patient. Fuck." He curses under his breath and drags his hand through his hair, disarranging it even more.

"I'm not a patient." The words escape me because watching him chastise himself feels like ten kinds of wrong.

I should be the one holding the whip.

"That's very kind of you, Lussi." He pulls his shoulders back straighter. "It was still inexcusable, my kissing your hand. I'm sorry."

But I'm caught on his initial description. A thrill of something I can't name tap dances over my chest and zips through my veins. No one has ever called me *kind* before.

"It's fine," I find myself saying. "No harm done."

He clears his throat, flits his gaze to the ceiling, and sighs. "Regardless, I really do think you should consider therapy." He raises his hand at my instinctive step back. "I'm sure not everyone can recognize your suffering, but I've treated many people with similar afflictions whose lives are lessened by their need to make the world perfect. With so much chaos now..."

"In Norway? Is this chaos in Norway?" I take a half-step toward him. Have I been missing something?

"Er, yes. I suppose. It's everywhere. It's a mental chaos, not a physical one, though I suppose the physical will naturally follow. The point is, people no longer know what to believe or who to believe in, and the more chaotic the world, the greater the desire to control as much of it as one might. In a way, not suffering from OCD is a little bit insane."

Which is precisely how I feel. It's true that in the bigger cities the messes are so enormous, I no longer bother trying to right them. I send my horde to wreak vengeance, but when was the last time I took a personal hand?

I suppose it's true that the chaos has been overwhelming. The only way to deal with it, even for me, is not to deal with it. If I don't see it, I won't have to organize it.

A small roll of disquiet runs through me. Could Nicholas Frye be right? Do I suffer from this OCD, as he suggests? Obsessive-compulsive-disorder. There's disorder in the very name. The fact the condition might point to me in any manner raises my rage.

I was born of a curse to make the world right. To create *order* of *disorder.*

No, Nicholas Frye, with his half-eaten pizza shoved precariously off the edge of the table, can no more understand me and put me in one of his little boxes than I can comprehend how he lives in such squalor. He's wrong.

"When you arrived, I was trying to write a speech I'm supposed to give tomorrow at *The International Association of Psychological Researchers* convention. I was trying to figure out how to talk about the onslaught of the supernatural experiences bothering people now."

More rage floods me. I narrow my eyes. "I'm a bother?"

"No! No, not you," he explains quickly. "You're proof. You're extraordinary. And delightful. And... stunning."

Fine. I'm as susceptible to flattery as the next person, especially when the flatterer looks like him. Nicholas Frye is easy on the eyes.

Am I that shallow? Am I not killing him just because he's hot in a messy, complicated, intellectual, trim-hipped and broad-shouldered way?

Apparently.

His gaze heats on me, drops to my breasts, and zips back to my face. He shifts in his chair.

Good. The attraction is shared. It's not just words.

He clears his throat. "More people now than at any time since the Dark Ages believe in the supernatural. Many are turning to religion rather than the looser idea of spirituality that's been popular in the past few decades, I think because religions offer strict boundaries, answers, and laws that help create order out of disorder. So, in a way, you're in style... being supernatural, that is."

He appears to love lecturing. Normally, the trait would annoy me, but in this man, well, I wouldn't mind listening so long as we could get naked. There's something about his disorganized eyes, his rumpled hair, even the fact he smells like fir, like Jul, like wild forests in crisp winter. And he's clean, despite the tee shirt he wears, jeans, and the pull of fatigue around his eyes.

And his shoulders. I do love a pair of broad shoulders.

"I've never trusted power other than my own, Nicholas Frye. I just do my job."

"Exactly. The look he gives me says I've just confirmed his statement about loss of trust equaling a disorder.

I lift my hand. "No matter. Now, Nicholas Frye, if there's nothing else..."

So you'll be my patient?"

And there he goes, enraging me again. "No." I lift my hand higher.

He jumps to his feet, stepping so close, his hot breath brushes my forehead. He traps my hand in his. "Wait! Just...

wait." He bites his bottom lip. "Prove me wrong, Lussi. Prove you don't suffer from an obsessive-compulsive disorder. Sit down for a few sessions with me. My treat."

I'm afraid that it would be a treat, though probably mine. The idea of remaining close to Nicholas Frye is more tempting than ice cream, but that's also why I should kill him. He's taken his outward disorder and lodged it within me, so I feel all disjointed and jumbled. I hate this confusion. I hate not knowing if I should kill him or kiss him.

Kill him. Always a better answer. Just be done with the mess.

"What do you have to lose, Lussi?"

Everything. But I push the thought away since it's ridiculous.

But what I can't push away is the way my stomach cramps and my throat clamps shut at the idea he'll soon be worm food. It's... weird. I've killed attractive men before. But ridding the earth of Nicholas Frye feels... wrong.

Maybe I don't have to destroy him immediately. I could... wait. I could ease a few aches before I straighten the world again. Just so long as I take him out of it so he ceases to create his chaos in the country I'm sworn to put to order, does it matter if he goes to his grave or to my home below shell?

He's right about my loneliness and isolation. Except for Jólakötturinn, who returned to Iceland ages ago, I haven't had a real friend. Sami doesn't count. He's a demon, even if he's devoted.

The thought of Jólakötturinn cuts with a thousand blades. I miss my best friend. But maybe Nicholas Frye could take her place for a short while? He's clearly brave in standing up to me. I admire bravery. And he's intelligent. And toothsome. Devilishly compelling, actually, with his hazel eyes and mussy light-streaked brown hair. We might be friends... or more than friends.

A flash of icy fire wings up my spine. An uncomfortable fullness settles in my core as I study the man I should destroy.

I can't compel his service. There's still the matter of free will, though the way his gaze heats upon me and repeatedly strays to my breasts makes me think I may not need to work hard at convincing him of much. I've kidnapped others and left them far from their homes. I've never kidnapped one to keep in *my home.*

Yes. I like the idea. Keep a pet, kill him when he ceases to satisfy. Maybe. At least it's an option should he annoy me. "I'll make you a deal, Nicholas Frye."

He unclenches and looks at me with a glimmer of hope. "Anything."

Oh, the fool. I shake my head before I wrap my fingers in his mussy hair and yank—gently.

Mostly gently.

"*Oww!*"

I drop my hand. "That's to wake you up, you idiot. You never, ever say 'anything' to a supernatural. Were you born with a washed brain? Try again." But my touch softens as I stroke his hair back into place. The least I can do is help him overcome his tendency to trust, especially if he's going to help me while away the lonely hours in Hell.

Hell is not a place anyone should trust.

"I would be open to a deal, depending upon the terms," he says in a measured tone, drawing even closer. He's heat against my skin, though he doesn't touch me.

My hand falls to his chest. Under his sweater, muscles I didn't expect round under my fingers. I'm tall, but I come only to the underside of his chin. "Much better, human."

"I'm a fast learner."

Another pang centers at my core. I ignore it and step back a few inches. "That may save your life, Nicholas Frye."

"Nick."

"Nicholas Frye," I repeat, unwilling to give ground. "The deal is this: you may help me with this disorder you believe I suffer if you will accompany me back to my home and live with me for... let's say a year. If I haven't slayed you by the end of your indenture, I shall consider giving you your freedom."

If. Consider. These words negate any implied promise in my deal, but I already know he's too trusting, too… naive, to understand the danger. Then again, he doesn't have a lot of choice.

"A year? No. No way. I have patients and family." He begins to bluster, stepping back.

The loss of his closeness jumps into my bones.

He brings his palm to his forehead and closes his eyes. "Lussi, please. I can't leave my life for a year." Those beautiful eyes open as he begs. "My mother is all alone. I don't have any siblings. Have some compassion."

Oh. Right. His mother.

I can't take him away from his mother. I'm a monster, but I'm not monstrous, though I've taken other children from their parents. But never an only child, and the ones I've taken have been neglected, ill-treated, or raised in a pigsty filled with disease-ridden vermin. Taking them has been a benefit to their health and safety.

But Nicholas Frye has been loved and well-cared for, clearly. He's so trusting, he cannot have been anything but.

"My compassion is in not killing you now for keeping such a messy room, in which case she would never see you again. A year parted from her is better than an eternity." Though once again, those cats begin fighting in my chest. Damned cats.

Slowly, he sinks back down into his chair, his face ashen. "You would really kill me?"

Of course I would. But his forlorn look makes me even more uncomfortable, so I don't say so.

He squinches his eyes shut before opening them. "What would you expect of me throughout your year?"

"Does it matter, given death is the alternative?"

"No. I suppose not."

"Wrong!" I bend down and grab his face between my hands, all the prickly little stubble doing something weird to my equanimity once more. But when shock registers across his expression, I draw my hands back.

He really is too trusting. His lack of guile sends an odd emotion twisting up inside me. I feel unsettled and icky. The sensation is something similar to the bag of clawing cats, but different. It's itchy inside my veins. It's twisting my esophagus.

When I first came into being, I paid close attention to each emotion I felt. I haven't done so for a very long time, except for guilt, since that's a recent addition. Nicholas Frye is giving me oodles of feelings I can't yet comprehend.

I clear my throat over the lump that's grown there. "Wrong, Nicholas Frye. You shouldn't agree. I could plan to torture you for a year. I could remove your fingernails, strip your skin from your bones, and make you sleep with a herd of swamp demons. The year would feel like forever, and believe me, death would quickly seem preferable."

He pales further and wraps his hands around the glass to conceal their tremble. Three times, he tries to respond but loses his words. Finally, he manages, "Is that what you're going to do to me?"

"No." I back away slowly. "I'm just trying to…"

"Fix me," he says when my words stall. "I understand. I'm like a glass out of alignment."

And I'm suddenly very sure I'm making the wrong decision in letting him live.

CHAPTER SIX:

Lussi

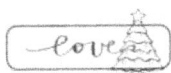

Nicholas Frye finishes my sentence, skipping right to the heart of what I am. "You're just trying to protect me from my own abysmal instincts. I'm guessing that's what you're doing with Norway, too, trying to protect your people from chaos, even if it means destroying some of them."

The earth shifts a little. Someone's vacuumed all the breath from my lungs. A strange ringing fills my ears.

He's not condemning me? Why not? I'm The Winter Witch of Norway. People hate and fear me. Always. They don't assign me decent motives. Even the woman whose curse gave me life never treated me with anything but trepidation and a healthy dose of disdain.

Focusing on his glass rather than the tumult of emotions falling through me, I send the crystal back onto the tray with my magick, clean and in alignment. Instantly, I feel better. I can breathe again.

I still have to swallow before I can speak. "You must learn to be less naïve in your pronouncements, Nicholas Frye. You've been sheltered, but words matter. Let yours be perfect lest they be used against you." I feel like a teacher, telling him what any child should know.

No wonder his life is so messy. No one has ever taught him to take control of his own speech, so how could he possibly understand why keeping his space pristine is necessary?

He wants me to care less about order. I want him to care more. We seem to be at an impasse, but... I'm not bored, and speaking with him now, I realize I have been.

Plus, if he annoys me too much, I can always throw him in a pit.

"May I call my mother and explain my absence? She'll worry."

"Do we have a deal?"

He nods. "I'll give you therapy. You allow me to live. No torture. And I get to say goodbye."

"No torture of any kind?"

"Of any kind, and I determine what is and isn't torture."

"Fine. No torture of any kind." A sudden welling of pride fills me. I like how he's glued me to the spot, even if it's to my disadvantage. "Deal."

"Deal," he repeats, but his voice shakes. He pushes back to his feet and walks to the bedside table where his cell phone rests. "I need to make arrangements."

Cell phones are interesting. They're similar to brain-to-brain transmission, but through a gadget instead of direct communication.

Once, mortals called upon gods for help. Now, they develop whatever they need by themselves.

He turns his back to me as he punches some buttons. I can hear the ring on the other side before a chipper woman's voice sings a greeting.

"Mom, it's me."

"Nicky, baby! How's the conference? Are you eating? And what time is it there?"

I listen closely. I never had a mother, not really. The woman who called me into existence created me for revenge, and revenge isn't the base of a nurturing relationship.

"Mom, listen. I don't have a lot of time." He half-rotates his head toward me before resuming his conversation. "I'm going to be out of touch for a while."

"Oh, Nick. Not at Christmas!"

"Mom. I'm sorry. Can't be helped. I'm, uh, treating a patient." He pauses. "Remember my theories? Well... I'm going to get proof."

I hear some rustling. A pause, then she says, "Are we talking about your theories on the supernatural being real?"

And by the delicate way Mrs. Frye clips her consonants, I realize she doesn't approve his theories. She thinks he's crazy. I don't blame her, really. I'm supernatural, and sometimes even I can barely credit the other creatures of my realm.

But still, it's interesting, isn't it, that he's been studying beings like me? It's almost as if he's been waiting to meet me.

Once more, a strange tidal wave of confusing and dichotomous emotions rolls through me. I'm not sure what to think of his research. I'm not sure I want to be the subject of some experiment. I'm not sure I like the intimation the Fates are involved.

Then again, he's going to be a pet. A companion. Or friend? Maybe the Fates didn't put me in his path. Maybe they put him in mine to finally alleviate some of my loneliness.

And who knows? Maybe he'll even help me with some of my more annoying tendencies? Not that I need his help, but sometimes, every so often, I wouldn't mind just sinking into bed without having to brush my teeth for four minutes before wiping down the sink or being able to read and hydrate without feeling obligated to center the glass after each sip on the coaster. I keep losing my spot in my books. It's distracting.

When I refocus on the conversation, Mrs. Frye's mama-senses have gone into overdrive. Nicholas is trying to explain about me, and she's hyperventilating, which I totally understand since I am a source of danger. I'm beginning to share her panic, so I tap him on the shoulder and hold out my hand for the phone.

Nicholas Frye is a long way from being a child. Children, I protect, though most people don't immediately recognize how taking them is protecting them. I don't protect adults. And yet, here I am, wanting to save Nicholas Frye from my killing impulses and his mother from her worry.

"What?" he mouths, brows raised. But the pain of what he's doing to his parent clouds his hazel eyes.

"Give me the phone."

"Why?"

With a sigh, I pluck it from his fingers with my magick.

"Lussi! Give me that," he hisses, swiping for the phone but missing. He's probably afraid I'll roast his mama.

I freeze him so he can't interrupt. "Hello, Mrs. Frye. I'm Lussi, The Winter Witch of Norway. You can find me on the internal net, though much of what is said of me will be lies. I read last year that my friend, Jólakötturinn, who you might know as the Icelandic Christmas Cat, ate sixty people, but I know for a fact that she hasn't eaten anyone in years."

I cross my fingers behind my back. Jólakötturinn *probably* hasn't eaten anyone because people nowadays buy new clothes at least once a year and she only eats them when they don't.

"Lussi. Please." Nicholas Frye is struggling to hold out his hand for his phone. His battle against my magick strains his features.

I shake my head and stick my tongue out at him. His eyes widen in shock.

He's going to be fun. "The point is, I'm the proof of the supernatural your son has been seeking. We've come to an agreement. If he learns his lessons, I'm hopeful you'll be able to see him in a year, and... hello?"

"I'm here." The words escape between staggered breaths that might be sobs. In a whisper, she adds, "Do you promise? His safety? Because he's my only child, and I can't..."

Can't finish her sentence, obviously. Not that it matters. I can't and won't promise Nicholas's safety. What is she thinking to ask me? She's just like her son—issuing a barrage of insistences where she has no claim.

My entire core winds up like a toy about to spring, but when Nick's face collapses in terror, I don't blast his mother through the phone.

"Lussi. Please." He begs in a way that makes me melt.

Poor Nicholas. He has so much to learn about prodding witches. I suppose he deserves some grace. Plus, he looks like a cartoon kitten, all wide, beseeching eyes and trembling lips. What fear he doesn't hold for himself, he's kept in abeyance for his mother.

I can respect that. Show me a man who loves his mother, and I'll show you a man with a good heart. "I'll care for him as best I can, Mrs. Frye. I hope we'll learn from each other."

"But he's…"

Reassuring anxious mothers isn't something I'm good at. "Yes. I know. Look, he'll be fine. Probably. I mean, it's Hell, so he'll have to make some smart choices, but still. He should be fine." Probably.

Releasing Nicholas Frye from his paralysis, I click off and throw the phone so it lands centered on a pillow. I've spent too much time in this room already. I've got people to slaughter, demons to rein in, and already the night is leaching into day. I'd like to be back through the portal before the sun crests, just in case the new king of Hell takes issue with my extending my night. The less interaction I have with that spawn of Heaven, the better.

"I'm running late, Nicholas Frye. We need to leave."

"Er..." He casts a glance at his phone and then his laptop.

Before he can ask, I send the items into his hands. "Yes, to answer your question, we're hooked up to 5G. The radiation is horrible for humans, but connectivity below shell isn't a problem."

"I need to contact my office. And the *IAPR*."

Fine. I wave my hand to let him know it's okay and focus upon my demons. He leaves voicemail messages and then does something on his computer.

Everything seems to be in order with my horde. They've caved roofs, killed a few people out of bed (and really, the only people out at three in the morning on my night in Norway can only be about nefarious business), and... stolen chickens?

"Put the chickens back, Rotten." I grit my teeth and shake my head. We don't disarrange animals. They're sacred.

Once I've checked with all my demons and sent further marching orders, I gaze around the room. It's tidier now but still disarranged. Leaving it a mess disturbs me, so I wave my hand. The covers smooth, the remaining garments fold or hang, and the dishes deposit themselves into the kitchen's sink. I wave away all the detritus of past meals until the room is straightened and made orderly.

There. I can breathe deeper.

Nicholas Frye is placing his computer and phone back in his bag. He picks up his mother's gifted sweater with his name sewn into the tag. With a small smile, I offer my palm to him. After only a slight hesitation, he takes it.

Brave. I like that about him. I like it a lot.

But for a moment, I'm the one who hesitates. I still have hours left in *Lussi Langnatt*. I could send Nicholas Frye onto my home, there to wait for me. That's what I should do, but for some inexplicable reason, I don't want to.

I don't want to enough so that I decide to call it a night rather than continue to oversee the straightening of my realm.

Three seconds later, we're in my bedroom in Hell. In another few moments, after I yank their cords, my demons pile in after us. Nicholas jumps and screams like a girl. But his blush the moment after as he catches my gaze sends warm bubbles sparkling through my chest.

I'm almost certain I've made the right decision to bring him to Hell.

Probably.

CHAPTER SEVEN:

Nicholas

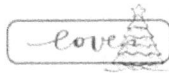

I'm in Hell.

Most people use those words in a figurative sense, but not me. I'm smack in the middle of the mythological realm, in The Winter Witch's bedroom.

And all my attention immediately hones in upon the bed. The covers are pure white and made of some sort of heavy silk embroidered in straight edges with silver thread. Each pillow lies squarely centered, seven in total, sitting three to each side in descending order of size. A single, longer rectangular one perches in the middle. I couldn't achieve such perfection with a measuring tape.

It's not a bed that encourages sex, which is a relief. I won't be imagining arousing Lussi with my tongue if I'm worried about staining the sheets. The last thing I need to do is overstep my professional boundaries. Starting now.

But I can't look away from the damned bed. It's like some sort of siren song. Cool sheets against Lussi's cooler flesh, heat rising like steam as I plunge inside her...

If she knew what I was thinking, she'd strike me dead.

Again, not a metaphor.

Forcing my gaze away, I surveil the rest of the spacious room. A crystal chandelier hangs from tall timbered ceilings of white-washed wood. Bleached wood floors sport a large white woven fur rug. Two comfortable, overstuffed gray silk chairs stand before a wide hearth composed of gray and white stone that sparkles with something like mica. Each chair has a matching footrest.

Other pale wood furnishings such as a small table and chairs, bureaus, a desk, a bookcase, and a chest of drawers bear rich patinas as if weathered by age in some sort of ultra-luxurious Scandi design. White flowers, fragrant and bursting with dew, give off a complicated and sensual fragrance.

If I stay too long in this pristine room with its clean edges and understated opulence that makes me want to throw The Winter Witch down and add some color to the space by forcing a blush to her cheeks, I won't be able to keep it together.

I look back at Lussi. Gray eyes, fair skin, an odd shade of hair, not quite white but not silver, either. The more I study her, the lovelier she becomes. She's like a work of art, absolute perfection in her contradiction of angles and curves.

Beneath her white gauze, she's got a stunning figure. My palms, with a mind of their own, keep urging me to reach out and smooth over her delicate shoulders, down her dancer's graceful arms, and over the hourglass shape she hides. Instead, I force my eyes away.

And center again on the bed.

Damn it!

The hearth. A blazing fire burns, which must be why beads of sweat have broken out along my forehead. The flames heat the room to roughly the temperature of the sun. I don't need the sweater my mother gave me that I managed to scoop up from the garbage bin before Lussi transported us in a whirl of nothingness.

But my thoughts and observations stall as demons pop into existence. They startle me so much, I yip in surprise.

Fine. I scream like a little girl. But I dare anyone not to when a good three dozen horrible-looking demons (think exposed bones, sagging gray skin, bloody warts, et cetera) appear out of nowhere and crowd the space. They wear matching scowls as they stalk around me, surrounding me in a tight ring, all of them oozing malevolence and violence.

Fine. Not looking at Lussi. Not asking for her help. I've stared down bullies before. Never thirty-plus of them at one time, but

I'm not a nerdy child anymore. I know how to fight. How bad could this get?

I try a friendly approach first. "Er, hello, gentleman." I lift my hand. "I'm Nick."

In response, one of them reaches out and pushes me before I can lock my legs. I go flying back, only to bang into other demons who push me forward.

"Vorvald! Regi! Did I say you could touch him?" Lussi parts the crowd like a hot knife through butter. She grabs the two offending demons by their hair and smashes their heads together. "That's three days in the Punishing for touching what isn't yours. Shogram."

"Yes, my lady?" Another demon, this one lanky and dark-haired, steps forward into the tiny center we're occupying.

But something strange is happening. When the demons first stumbled in, they were deformed, hideous monsters. But they've been reshaping before my eyes until they're gorgeous, like supermodels on magazine covers. All of them.

What the...?

"Shogram, escort Vorvald and Regi to the Punishing. Get a receipt this time and ask whoever's running things to kindly write in a neat and precise hand. The last time I sent Gorkurkus, I couldn't note the sentence in my calendar because I couldn't read it."

"Yes, my lady." One of the demons grabs the guys who pushed me by their elbows. Vorvold doesn't fight. He bobs his head, whispers an apology to Lussi, and allows the other demon to lead him from the room by the door at the far end of the wall. Regi, who's sent me a look promising pain, digs in his heels at first but swiftly staggers along.

"Nicholas Frye, are you injured?" Lussi leans into me, grabbing my attention. Her hand strokes down my chest to my abdomen.

Another four inches, and she'll touch me exactly where I need her most. Fire erupts under the weight of her palm. My mind blanks as I harden to roughly the consistency of steel. My breath falters when her fingers stroke lower, searching for injury.

I grab her wrist. "Fine. I'm fine, Lussi."

All three of her gray eyes grow wide. She glances where her fingers lie, and slowly, I let go.

"Be careful, Nicholas Frye. Hell is not for the weak."

"I'm not a wuss. I just didn't expect to be assaulted by form-changing demons."

"Expect it next time. Expect it always." She removes her hand and steps back, but behind the seriousness of her expression, I sense she's laughing at me.

I pat my shirt into place, trying to collect myself, only to jump again as Lussi waves her fingers. The heavy computer bag I've been carrying disappears, along with my sweater and cell phone.

"In the closet," she says before I can ask. She points to a whitewashed expanse of wood across from the bed. After barking out directions to the remaining demons, she waits for them to scatter before turning back to me. Her right brow is raised with anticipation.

Oh. Right. She asked a question. It was...

Laughing, she runs her fingertips over my jaw. I swear, I see stars.

I don't know what she makes of my swiftly indrawn breath, but her expression firms, and she drops her hand. "I asked if you wished to shower and change. It's late, and we should get some sleep."

In bed. I dart a look at the looming furniture, and more fire winds its way through me. "Um, here?"

"Are you afraid to sleep in the same bed with me, Nicholas Frye?" Her lips twist and laughter sparkles over her gray eyes.

"Not afraid. Professional." I put as much conviction as I can into the response, but the reedy quality of my voice gives the words a question.

She shrugs. "Sorry. No other quarters for you, at least, none where I can keep you safe. Safe-ish. Don't worry. I don't bite."

But judging by her expression, she might. And just the idea of her sinking those even teeth into my neck in a fit of passion makes my blood boil.

I'm used to lusting over interesting women. I'm a guy in my prime. If I'm not hard twelve times a day, I'm ill. But Lussi's effect on me is so much greater than seems reasonable.

Maybe she's a succubus?

"Are you a succubus?"

She laughs, a sound as light as chiming bells. "No. Poor things never get to have any fun." For a portentous moment, she leans closer until her breath skirts my jaw. "They perform their work through dreams."

Despite having hardened into steel, at her words, at her action, I fist my hands and manage not to grab her as she backs away. Instead, I trail her into a bathroom the size of a ballroom.

Marble and silver appointments command the space. An enormous round pool rests in the center of the room. At the far back, a shower stretches across the width, heads pointed in staggered rows. Two long marble counters with deep rectangular sinks line the other two walls. And on the expanse closest to the door through which we've just walked, two silver chaise lounges wait. They're too plush for a bathroom, but obviously, Lussi doesn't worry about wet and mildew like normal people.

Next to the long chairs are two matching closets. Lussi points to one. "That one will be yours. You'll find a robe inside. Oh, and..." She trills her fingers. Lines of glass jars appear among other glass jars along the shower wall. "In case you wish more masculine scents than the ones I use. I've tried to duplicate the one you're wearing now. I've added some other toiletries in the cabinets, there."

I nod, suddenly feeling like a female captured by an alien prince who intends to keep her in his harem. What have I done in giving myself over to Lussi's control?

My body doesn't seem to have a problem with my helplessness, even though I've never possessed a single submissive bone in my life. It's just not who I am. I'm the one in control. Always. However, apparently no one told my dick. It's pulsing with joy at being held captive. Lussi's captive. In Hell. With demons.

I knew I could fall for a dangerous woman. The adrenalin and need rushing through me is like a runner's high. My body is all in for whatever adventure I find.

Except my brain. My brain knows I'm in trouble.

***

The shower both mellows and revives me even further, as does the goblet of white wine that appears on the shelf by my elbow, resting just outside the spray of water. After drying off on the softest white towel I've ever felt—think baby puppies mixed with long-furred kittens—I slip into a pristine white linen priest's cassock with a Nehru collar.

Lussi must have grabbed it from the closet for me, not trusting me to find it, because it was laid out and centered at perfect angles on the chaise lounge. No underwear, though, and the further confirmation of her control ices my veins again.

Forget my earlier sense of adventure. I'm a dominant sort of guy. I don't mind foregoing underwear and letting my dick swing free, but I want it to be my decision. I think.

Even the robe... I can't help wondering if Lussi has dressed me this way for easy access, to keep my mind pure, or simply because robes are fashionable in Hell. I don't know, and what I don't know might very well end in my death. Or worse.

Come on, Nick. Don't be a wuss. You're not some helpless maiden whose virginity is being threatened.

If Lussi insists on using me as her new sex toy, I can't honestly say I'll object too strenuously—or at all. Lusting for the chance to offer up my body for her pleasure might be a better description of my response. All those curves and angles, and those lips...

And look at my brain, following in my body's wayward downhill slide.

Nope. No way. Despite my obvious attraction to her, I made a deal to provide professional services. Professional therapist-patient relationships do not begin with sex. Or sleeping in the same bed.

Then again, they also don't usually begin with being kidnapped.

The lack of certainty as to what Lussi intends and what I'll manage to fend off, since I don't want to fend her off, is driving me nuts.

Fine. I'll call the situation a growth experience. That which doesn't kill me will most certainly make me stronger.

But when I brush back my hair with a gold comb I find in the drawers beneath the row of sinks, I see the war of hesitation and desire playing out on my face. Under my damp brown hair that curls against my forehead, my hazel eyes sparkle and my lips frown. Neither expression goes with the other. My stomach is turning, but I've never felt so free or so alive.

I've never been a man given to uncertainty. My usual calm, level-headed approach to life and problems has always served me well. I may be outwardly messy, but inwardly, I follow clear, straight paths to positive outcomes. Right now, though, I'm so twisted, someone could mistake me for a pretzel.

When I walk back into the bedroom Lussi is seated before the fire. Her silver-gray eyes darken as she watches me approach. When I'm about three feet away, I stop and gesture to the bathroom. "Thanks for the wine and, um, everything."

"You're very welcome, Nicholas Frye." She carefully marks her place in the book she's reading with a long strand of hard silver and places it on the small table next to the chair. Habit makes her center the book perfectly, but she still takes a moment to arrange the edges before she lifts to her feet. "Let's see what I have to work with."

Her sultry smile combined with the potential sexual innuendo stills me, but instead of cupping my dick as I expect (fine, as I hope), she brushes past me, so close that I can see her nipples pebble beneath her gauzy gown.

Everything in me crashes and rolls as I realize she intended to make her words ambivalent. I clear my throat, but my voice still emerges as a growl when I ask, "Baiting me, Lussi?"

She blinks up at me, the sexiest half-smile I've ever seen tipping her lips.

But neither of us makes a further move to engage. Instead, I trail her through the bathroom door again. When she pauses, I look around, trying to see through her eyes. Knowing I'd likely be tested, I placed my wet towel in the basket under the sink and made sure to cap the shower gel. The toothbrush and bottle of forest-scented cologne, I placed in the cabinet and out of view.

Fuck. The linen hand towels. I re-folded them, but they're not centered. With a small frown, she taps them into place.

I don't know whether I'm terrified or turned on. The strange combination is going to kill me even if she doesn't.

"Not terrible," she allows softly, blinking up at me. She's tall, but I'm still taller. Wider. Broader. And the desire to show her just how she fits against me is overwhelming.

"Men don't normally buy hand towels," I explain, to excuse my lack of precision.

"I'll give you bonus points for your efforts, then." She smiles up at me again, a flirtatious glimmer in her eyes, until I reach past her, deliberately invading her personal space. Her indrawn breath staggers in measured stages.

What I'm about to do is insane. I'm not sure if it's a desire to test her limits or put paid to my own existence, but something in me has clearly snapped.

I grab the three towels and crumple them in my fist. "First lesson, since I passed your test. It's your turn to pass mine." I throw them onto the floor, there to spread like decaying blossoms.

Her gasp of horror widens her three enormous eyes. She blinks up at me again. "You didn't."

"I did." Unable to restrain myself, even though my brain is sounding the alarm, I wrap my arm around her and turn her toward the door. "And you're going to leave them where they lie until tomorrow morning."

"I am not." Like a skittish mule, she digs in her heels, refusing to walk. She glances back at the mess and bites her bottom lip between her even, white teeth.

"In point of fact, you will." I rotate her so she faces me. "You can do anything you like, Winter Witch of Norway. I'm going to prove to you that you don't have to let your demons run your life. Er—in a colloquial sense, I mean. I'm not sure I understand your relationship with those actual demons just yet."

Some or all of whom she must have been intimate with, maybe still is. They're gorgeous, and blatantly sexual. As hideous as they were when they first entered is how stunning they were when they left.

"Trust me, Lussi," I say when she doesn't respond but keeps trying to look back at the towels. I've moved my body to block them. Unless she's willing to admit defeat this early in whatever game we're playing, she can't see them unless she tilts her head around me.

Her plump lip releases as a low whine escapes her throat. Unfortunately, the sound goes right to my dick, which in turn tents my robe even further.

She notices. Of course, she notices. Unlike the way her pupils widen or the pink flush that runs up her skin, my arousal can't be misunderstood.

Score one for me, I suppose, because I've drawn her attention away from the towels messing up her floor. It's the most interactive therapy I've ever provided and certainly not a method sanctioned by any state's psychology board.

"I'd apologize, but circumstances are largely beyond my control."

"Oh." Her breath fans my chest as she leans in before she straightens. "I, um, don't mind."

"I think I might. Or should." Taking advantage of the moment, I guide her back into her bedroom, where the enormous bed awaits. I turn her in my arms and press her close to my chest though I keep my hips flexed backward. And in blatant contradiction of my words, I fan my breath along the sensitive nape of her neck. "Professional, Lussi. That's what we're going to be."

She looks up at me, confusion written everywhere. I don't blame her since it's all I'm providing. "I guess I'll shower, then."

"But don't pick up the towels." I insist as she pulls away. As if I hold any power in this relationship.

To my surprise, she nods. "I can leave them."

"You can. You will."

"I can. I will." With another glance at my tent pole, she gestures towards the bed. "If you're tired, don't wait up for me. We'll discuss the parameters of our relationship in the morning."

It's almost dawn—or maybe it is dawn. I stayed up late working on my speech. When Lussi appeared, it was already the next day. "But the bed. I don't think we should..." I gesture as I lose my words.

A mischievous twinkle sparkles in her eyes. The third one on her forehead winks. "Don't worry, Nicholas Frye. I promise not to assault your virtue. Yet." With a laugh, she wiggles her fingers and creates a crystal decanter with one of those matching glasses upside down on top of it. She floats it towards the nightstand closest to where I stand. "Water, should you become thirsty."

"Now who's being naïve?"

Her brows lift in question.

I gesture to the bed. "You trust me not to attack you while you sleep?"

She bites her perfect bottom lip between her white teeth, a look of amusement passing over her features. "Nicholas Frye..." She huffs back whatever she intended to say, though I can read the words on her face: *You're an idiot, Nick, if you think I'm not the power here.*

Probably true. I am an idiot. Then again, she might be magick, but I'm built a lot stronger than she is. If I were the type who could take physical advantage of an unwilling woman, and if I managed to take her unaware, I could, theoretically, hurt her. Not that I would force myself on any woman, ever. I wouldn't. I'm not sure I could harm her even if she's harming me. That's not the way I was raised.

But should she just dismiss me so easily?

Maybe she knows my inward tapestry, somehow. Or maybe she's just that powerful that the moment I hypothetically touch her, she'll turn me into a frog.

I steel my shoulders. "You can't be sure, Lussi. You might think I'm not a risk, but I couldn't live with myself if I didn't advise you..."

"And that," she says, interrupting me, "is exactly why I know I'm safe. You can't stand not giving me warnings. You're not going to try to force yourself on me. Plus..."

"Plus, what?"

She shrugs. "You have a crystal-clear aura. A little pale yellow. A little pale green. But they're colors of a good heart and good intentions. Soothing."

I'm soothing. I probably am, which is what makes me a good therapist, but it's not exactly what men like to hear about themselves. Studly, would be better.

With a brief wish that I had taken myself in hand while I showered, I wait until I hear the sound of running water before I ignore her instructions in favor of investigating the room. I need distraction.

Some of the cabinets hold clothing very much like what she wore today, with shelves of shimmering undergarments that make my mouth water. I ignore those and examine the books. All the jackets have been turned inside out, their titles written on plain white backgrounds in brown ink with a decorative hand. They're arranged from largest to smallest. It's such an OCD way to arrange reading material, I can't help but smile.

But in the middle of my search, a jaw-breaking yawn interrupts me. I cover my mouth, but when another quickly follows, I give in.

Fine. I'll bed down next to the three-eyed Winter Witch, who may or may not want to kill me, fuck me, or receive therapy from me. I've just got to hope for a quick death should I slide towards her in my dreams. Extenuating circumstances and all.

But even as exhaustion claims me, I can't help smiling. I knew there was magick in the world. I'll be sleeping next to it.

CHAPTER EIGHT:

Lussi

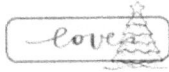

Nicholas Frye sleeps through the night, all tousled and gorgeous on my white pillowcases, his breathing even and deep. I watch as his eyes dart back and forth behind his closed lids.

I can't sleep. After showering, I slipped back into the room to find Morpheus had already taken my prisoner as his own. Trying not to wake him, I slid within the crisp, cool sheets and wiggled closer to his body. He gives off heat like he's made of fire, so of course I want to be near him.

But I don't actually touch him as the hours tick off on the clock because of consent. There's a firm rule all Kinds must obey about sexual involvement with humans, which is kind of crazy given we can kill and maim them pretty much at will with no one getting their knickers in a twist, except Lucifer. And even he'll allow it, under the right circumstances, like. *Lussi Langnatt*

I've never given the laws much thought since willing lovers haven't been difficult to find amongst the residents of Hell. Plus, humans are... delicate. I'm not one for rough sex, but I do appreciate bedding men I can't tear to pieces with a stray thought. I like being lusted over by someone who can throw me down and fuck me like he hates me, even while his hands and eyes are gentle and worshipful.

It's a lot to ask, and probably why I haven't found anyone in centuries to fulfill more than the most basic of my needs.

But Nicholas Frye... he looks at me the right way. I've already discovered a streak of kindness and goodness in him. Certainly, he has some delicious muscles I'd like to explore, not to mention a dominating tone and attitude that twists my core. He may only be human, but if I don't use my magick, he could be my Prince Charming.

But is he willing?

Well, not now. Now, he's asleep, but earlier, his robe tented nicely even though he kept yammering on about professionalism or some such nonsense. I couldn't quite tell the shape of his dick, but he's long. Wide enough to give me goosebumps? I don't know. But I could find out.

I close my eyes and try to force sleep, but I'm too keyed up. For the first time in forever, I sense possibility, as if maybe today will be different to all other days. For the first time in years, I have someone to share the hours with.

Outside the window, the night dwindles. Above and below shell, time flows differently, but Nicholas is still on above shell time. He needs his eight hours. Me? With my blood thrumming, it's hard to care about resting.

I won't touch him. I'm just going to run my hand over the top of the covers. There's a bedspread, thick down comforter, and sheet between my hand and his skin— and a robe if it hasn't snuck up around his waist as mine usually do.

Ooh, is he bareback against the sheets?

I push away the thought in favor of examining him. Strong, broad shoulders lead into well-muscled arms. He doesn't have those puny biceps like a lot of men. His are rounded stones like he works out with heavy weights and lifts Vikings for fun, but the rest of him is slim, so his physique isn't noticeable under his clothing. And his chest. There are divot lines between his pecs. The gown he wears has gotten stuck in one of them. I could pull it free...

A wave of heat sweeps over me. I pause to swallow.

Okay. Okay, narrow waist. Narrow hips, though I have to see him in memory since he's so covered right now. I can't measure his ass. Maybe later.

He turns onto his back, and I stop breathing. But look how strong that dick is. It lifts the weight of the covers, no problem, and seems centered on his body. That's a relief. I would have hated it if he swung to one side or the other.

"If you're going to explore further, I could help by pulling down the blankets."

My hand jerks away from where it's come to rest over his abdomen. Another second, and I would have touched his tent pole.

"That's the problem with sharing a bed," he murmurs, his voice all husky and growly, lined as it is with sleep.

And there goes my core, screwing so tight, I'm aching. I wiggle straighter until I'm sitting back against the pillows. "I, um- well, you see, I just wondered—er, yeah, oh! I wondered if you were too hot."

"Ah. So you were checking my temperature?"

I nod vigorously. "Exactly. I'm cold-blooded. Extremes in temperature don't bother me, but I keep my house warm, because, well…" Why do I keep it warm? I have no idea. It's an indulgence, having nothing to do with physical comfort.

"Because you've got a broad appreciation for things different from yourself."

"I do?"

"You must. After all, I'm the polar opposite of you—you can laugh at that dad joke, by the way—and here I am. In your bed." His hazel eyes sparkle, the colors lost between the light and his widening pupils. "Being appreciated, from my neck to my dick. You were going to explore my dick next, weren't you?"

"No."

He laughs, a dimple forming in his right cheek. "Liar." Struggling to sit up, he pushes back the covers in a messy pile of fabric. I'm so caught by the way his bare, muscled legs are revealed with his robe pushed up around his hips, just managing to cover crucial areas, I can't bring myself to care about straightening them. My breath stutters as my gaze drinks in his long, lean limbs.

Until he wiggles the fabric of his robe down so he's clothed to his knees. "First, good morning."

I nod, swallowing, or trying to. "Good morning."

"Second, we need to set some ground rules if our relationship is going to progress in a reasonable fashion."

"Right. You mean as my prisoner."

"*Tch.* No. As your *houseguest* and live-in therapist," he corrects. "I was considering the matter before you decided to, um, take my temperature."

"But you're..."

"Very attracted to you, Lussi. Obviously." He gestures towards his lap, where his prodigious member stands at attention. Perfectly, mouth-wateringly centered. "I can't hide my physical reactions when I'm near you, which is going to make a platonic relationship difficult. But necessary."

"Right. Necessary." I lick my lips.

He sighs and draws the covers back over his hips, hiding the part I'm staring at. "Trust is a requirement in a patient-therapist relationship, and if I'm sporting an erection, you're going to find it hard to trust me. I can't help my physical reaction to you, but I can help hide it by wearing jeans rather than a loose robe." He gazes down his length. "The robes reveal everything."

"I barely notice. It's not a problem. Really." Because I want him to keep looking like a sexy rumbled god in his robe. I like it. I like it a lot.

He smiles. I only know because he snaps his fingers. The sound startles me. "Eyes up here." He taps the spot over his nose and between his eyes.

And now I want to kiss him. He's got kissable lips, all plump but not overlarge.

Except—morning breath. Probably. Eww. I don't smell any offense yet, but I always make my bed partners brush and gargle before we fuck in the mornings, although honestly, I'm not sure I care with

Nicholas Frye. I think I might want to learn what he really tastes like.

Wow. That's odd. I'll blame it on lack of sleep.

"My attraction for you and your curiosity about me are perfectly natural, Lussi. We're two healthy specimens sharing a residence and, apparently, a bed."

Right. Words. Focus on words. "Do you truly mind the bed-sharing?" Because for the first time in my life, even though I couldn't sleep for examining him, I felt... not alone. There's comfort in a warm body encased in the same sheets.

"There's room for six on this mattress. I know people in the old days used to share sleeping surfaces without it being problematic." But his eyes pull down at the corners. "I'm just afraid that, a.—you might get the wrong idea, and, b.—I might accidentally roll over and into you."

I burst out laughing. "That would be some accident." I blink my eyes at him. "And not at all unwelcome, I've decided."

"Luss. Lussi." He threads his fingers through his hair, mussing the strands up even more. "Believe me, I've been thinking about this all night. You followed me into my dreams. But we can't enter into a sexual relationship while I'm your therapist. It wouldn't be proper."

"And you care about being proper?"

He nods, his features tightening as he exhales a long breath. "I care because if I don't, I'm jeopardizing the very thing I'm trying to do. I want to help you."

"Because I'm dangerous." It's not a question. I understand his motivations.

"Yes. Obviously. But also because you seem so..." He sighs. "I could have gone into accounting or law. I toyed with both, but in the end, I chose psychology because I have a knack of listening and drawing out motivations. I'm able to help people adjust to a harsh world and draw more pleasure from it. I want to do that with you because helping is important to me."

"Helping is important to me, too. I just have a different definition of help than you do."

He nods. "I respect that you're going to have different thoughts and experiences to what a human being might. I hope you can respect my perspective on the therapeutic process and the need to eliminate the sexual undertones between us as much as we possibly can. Once your therapy is complete, we can revisit the question of whether we want a different kind of relationship. But not until."

Oof. He's sexy when he's serious and laying down the law. Here he is, my prisoner—er, houseguest—and he's dictating what I can and can't do.

I can't touch him. Kiss him. Fuck him. And now I really want to seduce him into fucking me, probably because he says he won't.

Challenge accepted, Mr. Therapist.

He's still talking, probably making lists of what we shouldn't ever do and setting other ground rules, but I'm too busy wondering if I should just jump on him to see what he'll do next. I didn't kill him even though he's outrageously sloppy. Doesn't that entitle me to an orgasm? Or two?

All I hear is the ending. "Agreed?"

I guess I'll have to, but only because Hell's rules say I can't force him into a sexual union, though of course, I'm allowed to tempt him. Except, he doesn't want me to, and what he wants has quickly come to matter to me in a way it shouldn't.

Maybe it's just that I'm enjoying just being with him. Maybe I don't need to complicate matters with sex. If I do, I'll get bored of him, and right now I want to revel in not being alone.

I spring out of bed because he'll be upset if I "accidentally" roll over onto his dick. "Sure, yeah, agreed."

Without looking at him, I scramble into the bathroom. When I close the door, I lean back against it, my stability in complete shambles. Between my fast-beating heart and the way my blood pools in my core, I'm not sure that even the detachable shower head is going to help me maintain a façade of indifference.

Because I want *him*: his hands, his lips, his dick inside me, filling me. The trail of liquid seeping from between my thighs as I picture him kissing down my stomach and falling to his knees confirms I've caught lust. Bad.

But a tiny trickle of happy bubbles also flitters up inside me because along with all the things I'm not allowed to do, I can't help thinking Nicholas Frye wants me just as much. I don't know if his appreciation is for my body or all that I am, but the tiny, growing wet spot where the head of his penis was pushing against his robe before he blanketed himself means he's just as aroused as I am. It's not just an erection. It's a promise.

I rush through my ablutions even though I normally like to spend the morning taking a leisurely bath in my pool. I have things to do today. A prisoner—er, houseguest—to seduce without overtly seducing him. Punishments to be meted out, maybe, though I don't feel very much in a punishing mood. Therapy to sit through.

Actually, what I'd like to do is cede power to him for a bit. Just once, I'd like to be a regular female, spending a day with a hot guy and trying to get to know him.

By the time I return to the bedroom, I'm gratified to see Nicholas has made the bed. It isn't perfect. One side hangs lower than the other. There are unsightly wrinkles. The pillows are crooked. But he's tried. He's tried for me.

A thrill works its way up my spine. "Did you straighten this because you're afraid of me?"

Shaking his head, Nicholas smiles. "I should be, I suppose. I know you're dangerous, but... well, it's hard to be afraid of someone I've slept next to. No, I thought..." He glances at the bed and back to me, a light flush rouging his skin. "I thought that since I'm asking you to care less about making the world right, I should meet you halfway by trying to care more."

Yes, I'm melting. Sue me.

As I go around smoothing the rough edges, he takes the jeans and the shirt I magicked up for him into the bathroom, but he returns immediately. "When did you pick up the wet hand towels?"

Oh. Right. I did pick those up. But that's not a sign of OCD. Who wants wet towels on the floor?

"Once you fell asleep," I admit, heat flushing over my face even though I know I'm right and he's a pig.

But instead of the disappointment I expect to see, delight washes over his features. "Really? That's excellent. Progress already. I was certain you would clean the mess up thirty seconds after I left it. Huh."

His approbation fills me with happy bubbles. "Just meeting you halfway, as you said."

His slow smile is like a reward. "That's my good girl."

And it's a lucky thing he turns away and can't see the way my legs wobble. I flop down on the bed, melted, caverning, and needy. *Good girl.* Two words I should find insulting. Instead... *oof.*

CHAPTER NINE:

Lussi

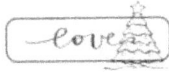

"So, do you work out?" I manage to slip in the question between pointing out the various sections of the forest around my home.

Fine. I'm a little obsessed with his body. Who wouldn't be? With those jeans riding low on his narrow hips and his long legs ending in boots, I need some distraction from what's below his belt. His biceps serve.

"Constantly. I was born with wide shoulders, but I was skinny and weak, which made me a target. Every bully in the tri-state area wanted to have a go at beating me up. Once I discovered running and weights, everything changed. No fights since my senior year of high school when I bulked out. Of course, that might also have something to do with growing older. Adults rarely pummel each other, not for lunch money, at least."

My heart squeezes as I picture little Nicholas Frye: thin as a rail, all mesmerizing eyes and sweet expression. It's human nature to try to destroy goodness, and he's a man who radiates it.

"Silver linings all around, though. I'm stronger and healthier than I might have been otherwise." But his voice lowers as he leans down and feathers his fingers over the raked stone path.

I feel those long digits sweeping over my skin.

Fifteen hundred years, and I've never felt a desire this strong. I don't need to down a few alcoholic drinks first. I don't need him to actually stroke me to make my body purr.

"Did you align all these stones?" There's wonder in his voice, even though I'm sure he thinks my path is excessively trimmed.

"No. Of course not." My horde did the work. I supervised. Tidied edges. Flipped stones to their better side. Arranged the varied white tones in a pleasing pattern of straight lines.

The look he sends me tells me he knows I'm waffling with the truth, but he doesn't say anything as he stands and brushes his long fingers against his pant leg.

He's wearing a dark green shirt and a pair of jeans I magicked for him based on what's lying in his suitcase, wrinkled. I could have ironed his clothes, but magicking something for him gave me an unanticipated thrill. It must be what little girls feel like when they dress their dolls.

Although, dolls don't have bulges—naked bulges, since I didn't magick him underpants—and I'm pretty sure it's the idea of my creation lying flat against his body that excites me.

"This is amazing, Lussi." He gestures to the forest and my path through to its center. "No wonder you prefer to remain here most of the year."

The footway appears to meander. In truth, it's meticulously laid out in a stylized pattern of "8s" that leads to a waterfall with a hidden grotto. Flowering bushes and trees spring a riot of color over the green and brown woods. I tried to lay out the foliage in colored blocks, but nature kept interfering. Blown buds took root, and before I knew it, there was pink in my red and white in my yellow.

I've left it as it wishes to be left because for reasons I can't explain, I don't mind the disorder in nature. It... balances.

Of course, Nicholas Frye notices the disarray. There's a question in the way he looks at me.

I choose not to answer it. "I've got something magnificent to show you." I grab his hand and drag him further down the path, ignoring the fluttering of fireflies racing up my arm from the warmth of his palm against mine.

When he squeezes my hand, a heaviness settles between my thighs. If he gives me another "good girl" right now, I'll do anything he wants. Actually, with another "good girl," he'll have to beg me to stop.

When we reach the fall of water, we pause.

"Wow." A slow whistle slips through his lips as he gazes at the majestic formation. He shakes his head. "I thought Hell would be all fire and brimstone."

"Quite a bit of it is. I wasn't around before Lucifer took the throne, but I hear he re-created the world below shell to mirror the one above. The worst parts, though, what you're imagining, still exist in the Punishing. Think of it as the ultimate gated community into which you should fervently hope to be denied entrée."

He laughs and pulls me into him before wrapping his arm around my waist. I'm sure he means it as a companionable gesture because I've already discovered he's warm and likes to touch, but what the simple act does to my insides can't be explained without talking about volcanoes, earthquakes, and eclipses of the sun.

I don't want to pull away. I don't care about the stupid waterfall I've seen a million times, but something in me hesitates to cross the line he's drawn and make the moment about my spiraling libido rather than his awe of nature.

Counting to five, I straighten. He drops his arm. Not with a single gesture or expression does he let on that he knows what his touch does to me, so why do I think he's noting the heat in my cheeks and the way I'm rigid with repressed desire?

I'm giving him too much credit, maybe.

As if to affirm he's only reacting to the stunning beauty of the forest and water, he grabs my hand again, swinging it like a child. "Shall we?" With his free hand, he gestures towards the falls where the earth and rocks descend to a flat pebble beach along the rim of water.

Surely, no one can be so oblivious, right? He must know what he's doing to me.

The trickling waters sing a calming lullaby. When we reach the bank, I pull him around the edge of the crystal blue expanse and through two large stones. The entrance to the cavern behind the waterfall is masked by the rocks. It's a secret I discovered in my first hundred years. Only my trusted servant, Sami, knows of its existence.

And now Nicholas Frye. I hope he understands how important it is, my sharing my secret with him. But how could he if I don't tell him?

"No one except Sami, and now you, know of this place."

His gaze is running over everything he can see, which isn't much since there's little light. When he finds me, he sends me a small smile. "I'm honored, Lussi. Thank you for showing me."

Another warm bubble of contentment wraps me in honey. "Wait."

I flicker my fingers and light the candles Sami placed on my order. They flicker in the damp grotto, on shelves, along the walls, and on wooden floats in the circular ditch of water towards the back. They're arranged in neat lines, except for those floating. I flick my fingers again and space those out, holding them apart with the merest trickle of magick.

Nicholas Frye gapes and blinks. It's not a great look on him, but the flames flaring in his eyes when he looks back at me makes the dumbfounded appearance bearable. "You did this? For me?"

"Yes. I thought we could lunch here while you work your wiles."

He blinks again until a small, slow smile tips up his lips. His shoulders settle. "By wiles, you mean therapy, obviously."

"If you say so."

For a moment, I think he's going to step into me, the way his eyes burn, but then his face firms. "I do."

Another shiver electrifies up my spine and down between my legs. I love it when he tries to be controlling. "And do I get to learn about you in return, Nicholas Frye?"

"Just Nicholas. Nick will do. It's what my friends call me."

"Does that mean I'm your friend?"

"Patient, at the moment, but..."

"But... more?" I lower my gaze to his bulge pushing at the unforgiving fabric of his jeans.

"Up here, Lussi." He gestures to his eyes, but there's laughter in them. "You're trying to derail your therapy. Avoidance. It's a common tactic, actually."

I step into him. "What is? Flirting with you? Threatening you with death? Sleeping with you?"

"*Sleeping*," he agrees, enunciating the word, "in the same bed, but yes. Technically, all three of those." He chuckles. "But allow me to pretend to be professional in the most unprofessional and romantic setting I've ever stepped foot into."

"But after I'm well?" I walk my fingers up his sculpted abs and bat my lashes.

But he only grabs my fingers in his. "As I said, afterward, we can decide what we'll be, assuming both of us are interested in being more. Until then, we're not going to cross any boundaries."

But beneath his continued attempt at dominance, I sense something I can't quite decipher. A seriousness, maybe, as if he's telling the truth about what he wants. His emphasis on *assuming* sounds an awful lot like *assuming the impossible*.

All my happy bubbles and warm honeyed contentment are swallowed up by something sharp, ragged, and heavy. I thought he wanted me, like I want him. I assumed we'd dance around sex until one of us gave in, namely him, maybe after we learned more about each other. I suppose I've been assuming we'll create a friendship that will serve as a firm foundation for great sex. Friends with lots and lots of benefits.

But... what if all he really wants to do is treat me? What if he's just one of those guys who springs erect at every breath of wind, and I've mistaken his attraction to me? In Hell, there are millions who'll fuck a light post if it smells good.

Maybe I am naïve. With the way he looks, he must have swarms of girlfriends. He's so sweet, he must have tons of friends. He doesn't need me.

Not the way I'm already coming to need him.

Tears push at my lids, but I don't understand why, not really.

Because you thought he could be your... companion. Your new best friend. Under all the heat, you thought he might genuinely be starting to like you.

But I have other friends. I don't need him, not really. I have Jólakötturinn. Sure, she's in Iceland, and I haven't seen her in years, but she counts. And there's Sami.

Except, Sami's a demon. Demons definitely don't count.

"Lussi." A wealth of sadness fills Nicholas's voice. He must see into my head with his own kind of therapist magick.

"That's okay." I sniff. "I mean, yes, I agree. Of course."

With a sigh, he wraps his arms around me and draws me into him. I can feel his heart beating beneath my cheek as he presses my head to his chest. Steady. Strong. Just like him.

"I'm not sure what you're thinking to make you look so sad, but I'm asking you to just... wait. The future isn't written. What we might become will figure itself out. Right now, I just want to focus on being your therapist, okay? Not for any devious reason. Not to hurt you in any way. And not because I'm rejecting you. It's just that the therapist-patient relationship is the only one that makes sense at the moment."

I pull back and search his expression, looking for some tell that he's hiding more. "Are you only pretending to like me? Because you're scared of me?"

"No!" He pauses. "No. I won't deny you're dangerous. I'm aware of the fact your temper could destroy me, but... I want to be here." He sighs. "That's all I can say right now."

"You do? Want to be here? Even though you're my prisoner?"

"Houseguest." He wraps a hand into my hair and tilts my head up so he can look into my eyes. "And yes, I want to be here, so much more than seems wise or possible, especially on such short acquaintance."

His face holds creases of worry around his eyes and across his forehead. I trace my thumbs over them, trying to smooth them out. Now he's the one looking sad, while I feel ten kinds of lighter inside. "I understand. We'll wait to be friends until after you've cured me of OCD." Which could take forever, so I'd better get started getting cured fast.

"Yes. After a cure. Although..." He pauses and looks up at the cavern's ceiling as if searching for words, or maybe whether or not to say them. With a little shrug, he adds, "I suppose that if your therapy progresses sufficiently, I may be able to hand off your treatment to a colleague, someone who's not attrac...er, a prisoner. Um-houseguest."

"Is curing me really so important?" Daunting thought, because shouldn't I be enough just the way I am?

"It's everything." And before my heart can stumble into a nosedive again, he adds, "You're so perfect, so amazing, that the little spot of ink in all your light is driving me crazy. I hate that you're ever discontent. I honestly believe you can be happier if you can learn to let the little distractions and messes go."

"So, my therapy is about making you less crazy?"

"Both of us less crazy." But he doesn't sound so certain. "What's not helping is sleeping in your bed and sharing romantic picnics under waterfalls." He gestures to the blanket and basket I asked Sami to bring. "None of this is a good idea. We're both getting ahead of ourselves." He pauses again. "Maybe I should leave."

"No!" I grab his arms as if to physically keep him in place. "No, I won't let you go. You're my prisoner, Nicholas Frye. For a full year."

He laughs, but the sound is ragged. He brings his palms up and cups my face, staring into my lower two eyes. "This is such a mistake, Lussi. If I do more damage than healing, I'll never forgive myself. There's a reason psychologists don't treat patients they're attracted to. There's a bigger reason why they don't live with them, sleep in their beds, or go on romantic outings with them. I need you to help me keep a professional distance, okay?"

I don't understand dreams, but right now, I think I might be living in one, one I'm not sure will have a happy ending or trap me in a nightmare. Never have my emotions jumped from one extreme to the other so quickly.

My throat clogs with words I want to say to convince him his stupid rules are just that—stupid. But I can't because I can see the war on his face, and I don't want to make him do anything that he'll regret.

I slip out of his grasp. "Houseguest, not prisoner."

"See? Progress already."

"And friends." I can't help but push.

He moves into me again and presses a kiss on either side of my third eye. "Fine. Friends."

"With benefits?"

He laughs and slaps my bottom. All of me crashes into the most insane burst of lust I've ever experienced. "You're incorrigible. Now, be a good girl and feed me."

Friends with benefits. Friends who are exclusive, maybe. We can decide what we want to be to each other once his silly requirements are concluded. He doesn't realize how quickly I can adapt to any situation. Perfect mental health? I'm already there.

We drop onto the spread blanket with the basket between us. Dipping into it, I withdraw containers and arrange them in rows along the edge farthest from the fall of water. It's so loud near the splashing that I can't hear myself think. I swish my fingers and stop the flow.

Ah. Better.

"Fuck," Nicholas whispers, gaping at the static sheet of water. He shakes his head. "At least I don't have to shout anymore."

I finish lining up glass containers and set our places so the knives mirror the forks, and everything is centered between us. I set a beautiful table, even on hard stone and linen. In fact...I flicker my fingers again and create giant soft cushions beneath us. No sense losing feeling in our butts.

But my goodwill is ruined when Nicholas Frye—Nick—scoops up one of the boxes and places it on the other side of the blanket.

I don't even think. I just wave it back into place with my magick.

"Nope." He waggles his finger back and forth. "Naughty girl. I want the box here." He picks it up and puts it down again off center, completely disarranging the harmony I've created. "And since we're two companions sharing a meal in a beautiful setting, shouldn't I have an equal say in how the table is arranged?"

"No."

Shoot. Too fast. He raises an eyebrow.

"I mean, yes, of course you do. Ordinarily. It's just, um, this side of the blanket isn't good for the boxes because of the waterfall. The food will get wet."

I'm congratulating myself on my ingenious response, one he can't argue with, when he points out, "But you've stopped the waterfall, so there's no spray."

Oh.

"Which," he continues, "is so impressive, I'm still stunned down to my toes."

Now, I can preen. Nicholas Frye—Nick—thinks my magick is impressive, which in turn means he thinks I'm impressive. Maybe dangerous and deadly, but not an object of hate or someone to be avoided. Impressive.

Warm lights shudder up and down my veins. For a second, I forget about the box.

Until my fingers crawl towards it.

"Lussi!" Nick's voice snaps with command, stilling my approach.

I draw back my hand. Guilt must be written all over my face, although I haven't done anything wrong. And damn it to Hell, I only want him more.

Red hot waves wash through my body. I'm suddenly aware of how his forest scent fills the space. Beneath my dress, my nipples harden into tiny buds. If I were wearing panties, they'd be ruined. And all from my name on his lips and the command in his voice.

"Leave the box alone for the entire meal, and I'll give you a reward." His tone is a silky whisper, seductive and enticing.

And I'm falling. I'm falling so hard and so fast, I can't catch my breath. "A reward?"

His smile has devil's edges. "One you'll appreciate. Deal?"

My gaze skims the box and returns to him. He's offering another deal to The Winter Witch of Norway. He's either ten kinds of fool or the bravest man above shell.

Or someone I could dream about, if I ever dreamed.

CHAPTER TEN:

Nicholas

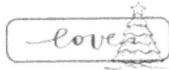

Despite my raging hormones, we manage to eat and converse. I don't think Lussi realizes how hopelessly twisted I've become. She's already got too much power in our relationship. I'm ready to give her more.

Fuck. *Relationship.* I can deny it to the moon and back, but here I am, smack in the middle of one, and we both know there's more between us than therapist and patient. Normal therapists don't promise unstated rewards for good behavior or pitch their voices low to slide under dresses.

What the hell am I doing, other than everything I vowed never to do? Any one of my colleagues would bring me up on ethics charges for how I flirt with The Winter Witch. The way I touch her with casual grazes of skin. The way I promise a future without promising one. But damn them all, they aren't her prisoner.

Houseguest. Prisoner. Fuck, does it matter?

Because if I'm honest with myself, and I usually try to be, I'm not attempting to seduce her in order to save myself anymore, if that was ever my real goal. She won't harm me. Even one short day in her company, I can see her temperament has been wildly exaggerated by myth. Maybe, once, she was a force of destructive nature, but if so, time has tempered her tendencies.

Sure, maybe she's destroyed homes, stolen children (did she steal children?), and killed those out of bed on the old Winter Solstice, but she isn't wonton in her violence. I've provoked her with intention, and instead of harming me, she's risen to the challenge.

Even now, she's resisting moving the box. She's admirable. She's strong.

And lonely. I can feel her loneliness like a damp blanket, and it makes me want to lean into her rather than away. She wears an air of vulnerability that challenges me to protect her, which has to be the stupidest thought I've ever had.

But am I fooling myself? Some sort of quick-fix Stockholm Syndrome?

I don't know. She's magick, and that changes everything. I can't watch her light candles, float objects, still falling water, and appear things like soaps, scents, and clothing, and not be captivated.

Plus, Hell isn't half as bad as rumored, and if the entire realm doesn't conform to what humans have been taught, why must the wide-eyed, lush woman conform to her myth?

The sound of singing birds wafts from the forest surrounding our cozy, storybook perch. Hell not only isn't terrible, it's beautiful. Elegant. Lovely and balmy. This is the place in which I can find boatloads of evidence to cement my theories into facts. And yet I don't feel like exploring any of the supernatural right now except as it pertains to Lussi. Whatever thoughts I'd had of offering her up as some type of proof of my theories have disappeared. I just want to understand her for myself.

Besides, I couldn't subject her to scrutiny any more than she could bring herself to kill me.

But I am going to cure her, and then... A groan escapes me at the impossibility of what I've set out to do. I've set an unreasonable goal.

"Oh, I should have mentioned that rockets are spicy. Here. Cucumbers in cream." Lussi hands me a bowl, mistaking my twisted expression. "People usually eat them together."

"Right." I accept the bowl, but when her fingers drift close to the unaligned box on the way back to her spoon, I have to conceal a snicker as a sneeze. Instead of touching the forbidden, she squares a plate of meat pies.

I don't ask what's inside them. Probably demon or orc flesh.

With a sharp look at my shiver, she draws back her hand.

I hide behind a sip of my wine, which is truly delicious. "So, if you don't mind my asking, how did you come to be The Winter Witch of Norway? Were you born to witch parents? Do witches get siphoned off to haunt different countries?"

She pauses with her spoon halfway to her mouth, an affronted look on her face. "I don't *haunt*. I *fix*." After dropping the utensil back on her plate, she wipes her mouth on her linen napkin, delicate as always, before continuing.

"I was born of a curse placed on the winter solstice in the year 524 of this era. I know this because the mother who cursed me into existence told me so when I returned from decimating the village next to hers with the intention of killing her, too.

I have no biological parents, witch or otherwise."

Unanticipated, sympathy tumbles into my chest like a weighted boulder. "I'm sorry. Does it bother you, not having parents?" Because when we first met and I told her I had a mother who would worry and miss me, her expression saddened. Lussi offered to talk to my mother. Insisted up it, actually. The unthinking empathy she displayed may mean I'm poking at a vulnerability now.

But instead of snapping, her gaze focuses inward. A soft smile touches her lips. "I do wonder sometimes what it would be like to have a family, a real family, especially during the winter festivities. *Jul*, Yule in English, what you call Christmas, has always been a sacred time. I'd like to experience the season around people who love me." She ruffles off the admission and sits straighter. "I find it difficult, being born of evil intent, of course, but anyone would."

"Because it makes you evil?"

She opens her mouth to deny it but shuts it before she can. Instead, she wipes her lips once more before carefully folding her napkin beside her plate. "Are you finished? Can we walk?"

And something tips inside me. I don't know what it is, but it's like a seesaw has just crashed down to one side.

"Luss?"

"Not everything is black and white, Nicholas Frye." But her face collapses. Her third eye shines with incipient tears.

What I feel in response is more than sympathy of her plight, or appreciation of her magick. It's... but I don't have the words. It's starlight breaking through a cloudy midnight, the moon glowing and lighting a path through a forest, a crisp autumn day in an apple orchard. The feeling is all those things and more.

It's her vulnerability set against the backdrop of her enormous power and the danger she emanates just breathing. It's the perfect storm of her guilt and her reason for existing. She's messing up my insides more than she can know. More than I understand.

Choosing my words carefully, I say, "Sometimes it's hard to differentiate being evil and doing evil. I imagine it's just as difficult distinguishing between fighting evil and being evil."

"I don't want to talk about this."

I've definitely touched a nerve. If she doesn't kill me now, she never will.

"Let's walk." I throw my napkin onto the blanket in a heap and jump to my feet before extending my hand to her. I'm a gentleman, I hope, but I also wish to distract her from the mess I've made.

Her gaze roves over the pile, but instead of correcting it, she slips her palm against mine and allows me to pull her to standing, I'm so filled with delight, it's like I just inhaled several cases of champagne bubbles.

"Fuck, Luss, you're so damned perfect I can't catch my breath." And because I'm ten kinds of idiot, even though I've just been counseling an arms' distance relationship, I throw caution and responsibility to the wind in favor of seduction.

"What are you doing?" She gapes up at me.

As she should. I'm turning tables, on her, on myself. I touch her cheek, tracing the soft ellipse of bone. The pale blush grows steadily stronger across her skin. If I was deliberately setting out to be a hypocritical and an unethical bastard, I couldn't be doing a better job.

But she's slipped under my skin, snuck up on me even while my defenses were at full strength. It's like I've been thinking I'm chugging non-alcoholic punch so as to keep my wits about me, and all along I've been downing Long Island Iced Tea by the gallon. I'm so unprepared for my reaction to her, or the way she's settled into my core, that I can't make myself act the way I should.

"I don't understand," she whispers, her fingers rising to cup mine as they slip to trace her jawline. "Didn't you just say...?"

I drop my hand and inhale a deep breath. I did just say.

At least she's ignoring my messy napkin. Unwinding Lussi's need for order by substituting a primal search for climax, arguably the most chaotic act in which beings engage, could be a brilliant scheme if done deliberately. But it's not. I just want her.

Emotion overruling logic, I pull her sharply against me. Her palms widen on my chest and she stares up at me, waiting. But all I do is spread my hand over her lower back, my pinky dipping dangerously near the split in her delicious ass. I lower my nose and brush it against hers, careful not to lean against her forehead where her third eye stares in confusion.

"You're not evil, Luss. I don't believe it, not for a minute."

"I'm not?" Her whisper rasps against my skin.

"You're a wild thunderstorm and lightning, but you lack the cold calculation necessary for true evil. You're heat and fire. Promise me you'll never think of yourself as evil again."

A shiver flutters over her skin. What I don't expect is how it jumps from her body to mine so that the electricity arcs and dives like a livewire through the pool of my flesh.

"I'll try."

My lips trace the contour of her hairline. I want to nuzzle into her, to breathe in her wildflower scent and swallow the arousal welling between us. "Succeed." And because I've already discovered her praise kink and know what it will do to her, I add, "Be my good girl, Lussi."

A little mewl leaves her lips.

Fuck. What the hell did I just do?

Before she can respond, I step away. Self-loathing fills me. I should be ignoring seduction, not trying to actively seduce her. Someone needs to take away my license.

Lussi stands there, wild-eyed, her hair floating up at the ends as if with static electricity. A whirlwind forms around her, a small tornado of desire. I don't answer it. Instead, I take another step back.

Her magick stutters and dies. She reaches out to me. "Wait, Nicholas—Nick. What about my surprise?"

I did promise, and she did leave the box alone for the entire picnic. "When we return from our stroll, I'll give it to you. Scouts honor." I raise two fingers up in the air. At her disappointed look, I add, "It's something better received sitting down than strolling."

She looks back at the blanket. With a mischievous smile, she retreats to her cushion and sinks to her glorious ass. "Then I choose sitting over strolling, Nichol—Nick." She's practically bobbing up and down with excitement. "I've never had a surprise. Not a nice one, anyway. What is it?"

Good question. I never imagined she could go so long without organizing her space, but luckily, I have an idea. It's reinforced by the tip of her silver-clad toe peeping out from beneath her pretzeled leg. "It is the best possible thing on earth. Can you get rid of all this?" I gesture to the food containers, plates, and the rest of the items that clutter the space.

With a wave of her fingers, they're gone.

"Thank you. You're so handy to have around."

Her smile is pure radiance at the tiny compliment, and my heart dips and stutters as I again recognize her essential loneliness. Sure, she can deconstruct an entire nation, but apparently, no one has ever told her she's awesome.

"My surprise?"

I move my cushion towards her and sit with my legs crossed. "Give me your feet."

Her brows raise practically to the level of her third eye, but slowly, she unwinds and stretches out her legs until her feet just brush my knees. She's wearing soft silver satin ballerina slippers that have no business traipsing about a forest. They match her gauzy silver dress with its undertones of blue and are just as impractical, but to my surprise, her shoes look almost new and not like they just hiked over wet stones and jagged inclines.

Taking my time, I caress the sides of her left foot with my thumbs as I move them to hook into the edges of the slipper. She hisses softly. She's going to be moaning for me soon in a way she shouldn't, but the sounds won't be nearly the cries I intend to pull from her in three hundred and sixty-four days' time.

There's no way I'm lasting that long.

I pull when I reach the heel of the shoe and remove the satin before dropping it over my shoulder, not caring where it lands. And Lussi, The Winter Witch with OCD? She doesn't even follow its path. Her eyes lock on mine, her breath held.

Perfect. I repeat the process with the other foot, and when both lie bare, I lift the first and shimmy closer so I can bend her knee and rest her heel upon my thigh. "My surprise is a foot rub. Do you like foot rubs?"

She shakes her head before shrugging. "I don't know. I've never had one, but-t-t—oh!"

I snicker as I push my thumbs into her arch. "Well, I think you're going to like this. If you don't, tell me and I'll stop. Okay?"

She nods vigorously and swallows but doesn't respond.

I wait until the first moan leaves her lips as I caress and massage. "Tell me more about the curse and how you were born."

"I-I, uh, was born of a curse. Oh, that feels so good."

"Tell me," I insist.

Another moan follows my words. She likes dominance, my dangerous witch. It makes sense. She's always been the ultimate power in her neighborhood. Those with strong personalities usually make either perfect doms or perfect subs. It can go either way.

Lucky for her, I'm a gentle sort of tyrant. I'm a dom, for certain, but I like my women to have their own desires, their own dreams, their own needs. I may prefer to be in control, but I'm willing to work within any boundaries I'm given.

And Lussi... she doesn't want or need to be overpowered, even were such a thing possible. I think she wants to release her loneliness onto someone who can bear the burden, maybe someone who can tempt and guide her into mind-blowing orgasms while respecting her power.

In three hundred sixty-four days, I'm more than willing to give it my best shot at being that person. Or sooner. Hopefully, sooner.

"Luss?"

"Luss," she repeats, voice soft. "I like the way you shorten my name." And another blush passes from her chest to her forehead.

"Good. Tell me about the curse," I repeat, to keep us both on track.

She nods, moans, and her lashes flutter, but eventually she responds. "Astrid Aggenson, a human witch, had a son she loved beyond all others. When the neighboring village came to raid, they strung him up, skinned and broken. That day, Astrid's entire village, livestock, and kin were either killed or kidnapped and taken as traels. Thralls—slaves," she explains when she notices my confusion. "Astrid escaped with only her youngest daughter, Sigrid, because they had been in the forests, gathering juniper with which to make ale. The best, she told me, grows near the pines."

I drop her foot and move to the other, there to begin with slow, light caresses, testing how ticklish she might be. I don't want her laughing. Yet. I don't want her mewling, either. My control has limits.

"When she could approach her son, Astrid cut him down and vowed over his destroyed corpse to avenge him. Though the longhouse had been set aflame, some cottages on the outskirts remained. She gathered the blood of the village's slain and mixed it in a cup, added the juniper that had saved her, and made her potion with a prayer to the old gods, the ones not named in any myth you'll ever read. But her beseeching did not work, as the sacrifice was not hers."

I stop kneading her flesh, a terrible presentiment welling up inside me.

She nods, reading my face. "Astrid began to work the spell again, repeating the words, using the herb. And for a sacrifice, she slit her daughter, Sigrid's, throat. She called for the old gods, the ones unnamed, to give her the weapon to set right the destruction. Then, overcome with grief, she sank into blackness. When she awakened, I was there with bloody hands and mouth, naked and pulsing with power. I had done my duty and avenged her son. What remained was to kill her, my maker."

"And did you?"

"Eventually."

The word sends ice down my spine. How easy she makes it to keep forgetting she's a killer.

Trying to ignore my disquiet, I begin massaging her foot again. A Lussi in a tizzy, I understand. I trust my powers of persuasion and her own common sense to calm her. A Lussi who puts off destruction until an opportune moment... for the first time since I arrived in Hell, true fear trickles through me. Is this what she means to do with me? Could she be evil after all, and I'm the one who's been seduced?

"After slaughtering the village, even the newly made thralls—remember, I was just born, and I hadn't yet learned temperance or balance—I was tired. And so, instead of killing Astrid, I lay down at her feet and fell into a deep sleep. When I awoke, she gathered me close and sang me songs, using the words of power that had pulled me from my sojourn in the Nothing. It was enough to settle me so I might learn what she had to teach. So I might survive. Why have you stopped? Is my surprise over?"

I shake my head and resume my caresses, working my way up her ankle to her calf. She moans loud and long as I dig my fingers into the taut muscles. "I was listening. How did you kill Astrid? When?"

She shrugs. "When it was time. When she no longer wished to live. In teaching me to survive, she found a purpose. I took her daughter's place in her life, though not her heart. She always longed for her true family. And so I killed her in an instant by snapping her neck when she asked death of me. Afterward, I laid her body in a grave of stones on top of a hill so the birds might find nourishment. Such were her wishes."

I don't know what to feel. It's a horrible story. My balls want to crawl back into the warm safety of my body, but at the same time, I'm so fucking sorry for Lussi, I want to rock her in my arms.

"Fuck, Luss. How did you deal with that? What did you feel?"

"Killing her, my maker?" Her eyes glass again as her face takes on a more distant look. "It was what she wished of me. I couldn't deny her simply because I would be alone once she'd gone."

Empathy makes me a good listener. A good therapist. But at the moment, it's tearing me apart.

As if she senses I can't continue with the massage, Lussi gently pulls away from my hands and wraps her legs back under her. "Thank you, Nick. That was a lovely surprise."

"Was it?" I can't even swallow. The words gutter on my lips.

"Yes. I can see why you're so proud of your profession and why you believe you can help me. You were right. Talking is freeing. I've always realized my past haunts me. How could it not? To my knowledge, I am a singularity, like no other living thing. Apart, I am The Winter Witch, and while over the years I've found companions, and sometimes even friends, nothing has ever taken the sadness of my beginnings from my heart."

I nod. I still can't swallow.

Lussi sighs. "Telling you, with your hands on my skin, with those unshed tears in your disorderly eyes, helps balance the loneliness I usually feel when I think of my origins. I can't explain how."

I can. It's not uncommon for a therapist to suggest, when all else fails, taking the bad memories and merging them with good ones. It's also why therapy works. Warm comfort, understanding, and acceptance take the sting from the hurt.

"If I'm helping you, Lussi, I'm glad." I try to work my emotions back under my skin before I ask, "But how did you become The Winter Witch and not just a curse?"

She smiles a soft smile before she slowly reaches towards me, very slowly, and caresses her fingers down the line of my jaw. "I was born on the Winter's Solstice, of course. My path toward righting wrongs was my inception. Lucifer watched me wreck my country for years before he restricted my reign of terror to one night. Maybe he saw I was lonely, because he assigned demons to my charge. I'm supposed to keep them out of trouble.

A snort of disbelief escapes me.

"The Devil isn't the terrible entity most people believe, but he clearly lacks omniscience."

"You... like him?" Satan?

She nods. "I feel a strange kinship with him. He, too, is hated. He, too, has been made to stand at the opposite side of good." She smiles. "He's always been very kind to me."

And that she could find Satan comforting illustrates how lonely she's been.

I lay my hands on her knees, needing to be close to her. It's unprofessional of me, like everything I've been doing and saying since I met her, but for the moment, I don't care. I need to touch her. She needs to be touched.

And in a move that surprises even me, one that should see my license yanked yet again, I grab her fingers and turn her palm towards my lips. In the center, I press a scalding kiss. My eyes close as I sink into the connection.

I'm so close to losing control that I can taste defeat, and I didn't even realize I was at war.

CHAPTER ELEVEN:

Nicholas

—*love*

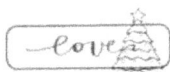

Over the next few weeks, our days lengthen into a companionable rhythm. Every morning, I wake with my body spooned around Lussi's delicate frame despite my nightly resolve to keep my distance. My dick remains permanently hard and aching, though I manage not to act to appease it.

Instead, I run through the perimeter forest paths and around the lanes of the quaint village in which she lives, hoping to exhaust my randy urges. While I'm out, Lussi bathes in her deep blue pool so that when I return and shower, the scent of wildflowers surrounds me.

I take long showers, as cold as I can stand them.

Afterward, we breakfast either before the hearth or outdoors in a tiny flowered courtyard. Beyond the lush garden, the forest flows into wilder and wilder woods. For all that the village center lies no more than a ten-minute walk away, the only sounds that intrude are those that nature provides. Birds and fluffy animals I can't name pad about and beg for scraps. The inner sun trickles light as cool breezes taper into warmer afternoons.

Honestly, Lussi's home is like a resort hotel. Staying with her is less hardship than reward. There's peace in Hell, at least in the parts she's shown me.

She's taken me to lots of places. Lussi, I've discovered, has no purpose other than her one night of destruction. It leaves her open and willing to participate in any activity I suggest. To keep my dick in my pants, or under my robe, since she likes dressing me in robes despite my erection problem, I suggest a lot of outings.

Once we finish our leisurely meal, we usually go for a walk, meandering over fields and forests. Sometimes, her demon hordes follow in our wake. She's asked them to give her space, but I don't think the thirty or so supermodels understand the concept. Still, they make adequate chaperones, and for that, I'm grateful. I'm too close to ruining everything.

And after lunch, we read. I play with my speech that I've not shown up for, though I emailed the host of the *IAPR* and explained that I'd been hospitalized with a dread illness. They were sympathetic and assured me of my spot for next year.

Since I'm not sure I'll be alive next year, I ignore their promises.

Most of my time is spent making notes about The Winter Witch of Norway. In slews of typed pages that I don't bother to number, I record her responses to the innumerable questions I ask. She doesn't seem to mind that I study her. She doesn't seem to like it, either, but she's been a good sport.

She's even allowed me to photograph her with the camera on my phone. Surprisingly, I get reception, and I've been able to call my mother and assure her I'm well. I sent her some of the photos, and she commented back about what a lovely girl Lussi is, how happy she is I'm finally settling down with someone, and, oh, by the way, the local hospital has wonderful plastic surgeons that can do something about the unusual birthmark on Lussi's forehead.

Lussi laughed when I told her.

But today, her mood is different. She's quieter than normal, more pensive. She appears distracted or introspective, but I can't tell what she's thinking.

We're picnicking on the Sea of Elicher. It's a wide ocean of white-spumed waves rippling over clear blue waters, a sort of combination of the Atlantic Ocean and the Mediterranean Sea. Around the edges, red brimstone cliffs reach to the sun-like light. It's hard to believe we're beneath the ground.

"It's beautiful, isn't it?" Lussi sighs and leans her chin into her hand as she stares off into the expanse.

"Gorgeous." I'm not certain if I mean her or the view. To divert my thoughts, I ask, "You've lined up the sunscreen and the glasses." I nod toward the edge of the table she magicked into existence. The first thing she did when we sat down was to arrange the items in descending height along the side.

"Must we always do this?" she snaps.

Huh. Throughout our weeks together, she's been calm, accepting, and temperate as I test her with messes, point out when she's righting her world, and burrow deep into her thoughts as to why she's organizing. So far as I can tell, she just hates disorganization. I can't find a common thread to pull that might indicate a deeper psychosis.

I study her. She seems composed. Dressed in a long silver gauzy robe on top of a white one-piece bathing suit that she's created from a picture on the web, she's as lovely as ever. But there's a disturbance in her energy, something palpable.

"Luss?" I tilt my sunglasses down so I can see her over the rim. "What's wrong?"

"Nothing."

"Luss?"

She picks at the table edge, no longer content with the view, and glares at me. "Fine. You know what's wrong? You are, Nick. You leave messes everywhere and want me to do the same, which is ridiculous and demeaning and horrifying."

O. Kay.

She purses her lips, looking out to sea again before her eyes latch upon mine. "You're trying to make me lose the essence of myself, and I don't like it."

And there it is.

During the past couple of days, it's true that she's begun to resist in small ways, but this is our first direct confrontation. I'm actually glad to see it. Not only am I a sucker for dangerous women—and in a snit, there's no female more dangerous than The Winter Witch—but it's also progress.

"Straightening, organizing... these aren't the essence of who you are, Luss. They're crutches."

"Essence." Her eyes narrow further, shooting sparks.

"Why are you afraid to lose your crutches?"

If looks could kill, and honestly, I'm not sure hers can't, I'd be spatchcocked and roasted. "I'm not *afraid*, Nicholas Frye, and the desire to be neat and orderly is not a crutch. It's a lifestyle choice. It's who I am."

Back to my full name, as if I'm a toddler receiving a dressing down. "If you're not afraid, then what are you feeling?"

"Annoyance. With you. Which isn't promising for your continued longevity, is it?" She rushes to her feet and stares down at me with those ice-cold dagger eyes.

"I think I'm dead only if that's what you truly want."

"Right now, it is." She raises her hand, threatening me, but not a single part of me fears her. Nope. I fucking want to be inside her.

A need to feast upon her twisted lips and suck along all the spots hidden beneath her clothing nearly overwhelms me. But instead of acting on instinct, I manage to pile my elbows onto the table and lean toward her. "Resistance is good, Luss. It means we're progressing. Your emotional guards are throwing up defenses."

Her hand falters before sinking to her side. "What do you mean, *progressing?*"

"I'm threatening your innermost view of yourself, challenging your defenses, and you don't like it."

"I told you I don't like it." She taps her foot. "Not news, Nicholas Frye."

"No, it is." I squirm in my seat while I search for the right words. "When it comes to our psyches, we place our strongest soldiers right at the castle doors and deploy our weakest ones on the front lines." I gesture to the chair she's abandoned. "Please, Luss. Sit. Tell me what you're thinking. Feeling."

"I'm thinking and feeling how profoundly relaxing my life will become once I disembowel you, Nicholas Frye." She lifts a finger and in one swift motion swishes it in a line.

A burning cut blazes from my wrist to my elbow. Agony flares as my skin yawns wide, but no blood flows, as if she's cauterized the edges.

I gasp as a wave of nausea floods me. Excruciating pain takes away my breath. She's cut me to the bone. I can see the white through the tear of muscles and veins.

My bone. I shouldn't ever see my bone.

Somehow, I manage not to scream. But I also can't shut my mouth.

She's hurt me. She's really hurt me.

CHAPTER TWELVE:

Nick

love

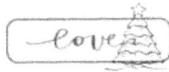

"Nick!" Judging by Lussi's expression, she's also shocked by what she's done. She stares at me, her hand pressed to her gaping mouth, giving every impression of being horrified. "Nick. Nick, I'm sorry, I..." She waves her hand.

Instantly, my skin re-knits. More slowly, the red line of the injury begins to fade until I'm left with nothing but the memory of a pain so profound, I'll never forget it.

"Nick. Please. I didn't mean—I was just so angry, and... I'm so sorry."

Just that easily, she could shred me to pieces. Logically, I knew she was dangerous. I just didn't understand how much. I didn't believe she'd hurt me.

"Nick, please!" She falls to her knees in front of me. Tears stream down her face, and a ragged sob emerges from her throat. "I didn't want...I d-don't w-want to harm you!"

But the faded physical evidence says otherwise. I flex my arm, testing to make certain everything has closed together properly.

Her sobs increase. She leans into herself, keening, until her forehead sweeps the ground.

The sound slithers up my spine. I want to tell her it's okay, but I can't, because it isn't. She hurt me. I was a fool to think I was safe with her. I'm not. No one is.

With some distant part of me, I'm aware she's speaking. The words are hard to make out through her crying, but I think she's saying, "Please don't leave me. I'm so sorry. Please don't leave me. Please."

And my stupid, treacherous heart breaks into a million tiny pieces.

I'm not aware that I've reached down for her until her hair sprawls over my lap, her cheek on my thigh, my fingers wrapped in her sun-warmed, silky silver hair as she begs, cries, and trembles, wetting my skin with her tears.

Her grief is more appropriate to a death. She's hollowing out, losing herself in her agony of what she's done. Of what I'll do in response.

Leave. I should leave.

But seeing her in pain, even though it's a result of her own deliberate action in cutting me, glues me to my chair. And my chest... my chest aches with a torment deeper than the physical one she caused.

"Sshh, Luss. I'm right here. I'm not leaving." But I have to reassure her for several minutes before her sobs lessen enough for her to hear me.

"Y-you're not?" She raises her ravaged face. She's not a pretty crier: reddened and widened nose, deep tracks under her three eyes, swollen cheeks. And yet, in this moment she's so beautiful, I can barely breathe.

Stockholm Syndrome, probably. My captor has deliberately injured me, and all I want to do is ease her sorrow. But logic has no place in my spiraling emotions.

Maybe it never did. "I should leave you, Lussi. What you just did to me is... unforgivable."

She wails again before she bites the sound back. More tears stream as she nods her agreement and clutches my thighs.

"Tissues?"

Her tears don't stop as she magicks a box into my hand. I rip open the top and hand her several, but when she merely scrunches them and sobs some more, I sigh and grab a few myself. More gently than I should, I wipe her cheeks and nose, then make her blow.

My actions calm her, at least enough so that I can converse with her like a rational inhuman being. "I'm horrified, Lussi, and... shaken... by the pain. By the fact you hurt me. You promised not to."

More wails sound, and she nods. I wait her out before mopping up her tears.

"I-I h-h-hate my-s-self. I-I'm s-so s-s-sorry!"

I brush back her hair, now more gray than silver, as if her emotional outburst has stolen her sparkle. "I'm glad you're sorry."

Something in my expression sets her off again. I wait out her sobs, and when they calm enough for her to blow her nose once more, I say, "If you ever hurt me like that again, I'll have no choice but to leave you. I can't stay with someone who'll hurt me. I'll go to my death first."

That's what I say. I don't know if my words are true, but I know that I should mean them, and that's enough to instill certainty into my voice.

She bobs her head. "I know. I know, Nick. I'm sorry. I don't understand why I lashed out like that. I... it hurts me, too. In here." She clasps her hand over her heart. "Never again. I swear it, Nick."

Back to the short form of my name. More progress, though the path is painful for the both of us.

"Can you t-trust m-me again?"

Can I? If any man or woman came to me and said their partner struck them, I would tell them that abuse is a deal breaker, to get out and run fast and far away from the abuser. Yes, sometimes people change, but it generally requires more than a mere promise to do so on the heels of delivering a strike.

But... this is Lussi. So far as I can tell, she's never had many real friends, though she often talks about the time she spent with the Christmas Cat of Iceland. She hasn't been socialized. No one has taught her to control her temper or to interact without striking out. In fact, she's been urged to let loose her wrath on *Lussi Langnatt.* She's less abuser than a child hitting or biting out of frustration.

Intolerable, what she's done. Intolerably stupid for me to excuse it.

Teaching her to restrain her impulses is my job, though, isn't it? Not the exact problem I wished to help her with, yet here I am. Plus, I can't leave her like this: broken, vulnerable, and at a crisis point because of my presence in her life asking her... forcing her... to change.

I can't deny I hold some blame.

A long sigh escapes me as I stroke her cheeks. "I need you to do something for me. Do you think you can?"

She nods quickly. "Anything."

The rash promise takes me aback. "I thought promising 'anything' was a bad idea?"

"It is. I don't care. Please, Nick. I need you to forgive me. Tell me what I should do."

"I hope it's that easy." I take a breath. "I need you to tell your inner battalions to stand down. They perceive me as an invader. I am, but you need to remind them that I'm not attempting to destroy the castle. Whatever damage I do in the short term, whatever chaos I create inside you, I'm only trying to fortify the walls."

"Yes. Yes, I will. I'll tell them. Absolutely." Her gaze darts past my shoulder as she takes a shuddering breath, her palms stroking aimlessly up and down my thighs. "I think—I've come to care for you a lot more than I should. I really, really like having you live with me. But that's also the problem, because I'm terrified that when you leave..." She stumbles into silence once more.

"Go on." But my heart is beating as fast as hers must be. "Whatever you're feeling, telling me is okay. I can handle it."

"Because you're strong. And brave. And you confront problems head-on. And I admire those qualities in you so much."

"I admire them in you, too."

She nods, gathering her courage before admitting, "I'm terrified that when you leave, I'm not going to be able to return to who I was before. If I give up my OCD, as you call it, I won't even have that crutch to sustain me. I'll just be an empty shell. If I don't have what I *was* and I don't have *you*, I won't have anything at all."

My heart quakes again. She's danger walking, sure, but she's also lonely, vulnerable, and weighed down by a horrendous origin story and a past she can't escape. Even for humans, it requires enormous strength to become someone we want to be rather than continuing to be who we've always been. Changing must be doubly hard for a being born of a magick curse and created to wreak violence and death.

Maybe I shouldn't be surprised she's lashed out, now. I should be surprised she hasn't lashed out before now. Plus, I've contributed to the unsteadiness Lussi's experiencing. Between the push-pull of attraction I'm feeling and manifesting, and the too-close nature of our situation, I'm not without reproach.

"I'm sorry, too, Luss."

Her forehead furrows in surprise. "You are? For what?"

My fingers smooth the wrinkles. "Sitting in judgment of someone else's actions and thoughts, beliefs and motivations, is a central part of my job. At an emotional distance, in a conventional therapeutic setting, it works."

"Like you're the king," she says softly.

"Yes, like that. I'm the king in my office, where my job demands I poke and prod, to lead patients to uncover, see, and acknowledge their disorders. But I've been trying to be king here, with you, while also becoming... friends." The truth of what I'm saying settles over me like a blanket. "That must be torture for you, to have a friend constantly draw attention to your foibles. And... confusing. Irritating."

"It has been torture, but it's also been... joy." After swiping underneath her eyes, she returns her palms to my legs. "I'm not as confused as you think. I realize you've been trying to help me, professionally. I've been trying to let you, but I'm also the one who insisted you live here with me."

True. "But it was my idea to try to cure you of your disorder."

She nods before sighing. "You were right about one thing. I am scared. Changing."

"Of course, you must be. But you're so much more than the curse, Luss. You're brave, beautiful, intelligent... amusing. I want you to be happy and... free." I place my palm against her heart. "I believe so strongly in your ability to be anyone, to do anything, I've overlooked the fact you might not believe in yourself."

"You believe in me?" She sniffs again and pats her nose with the tissue.

"I do." I quirk her a smile. "I'm not trying to change who you are, though. Not at all. You're... perfect. All I've been trying to do is help you overcome the need to fix the small things, the things that take time and attention away from your greater purpose. Although, if I'm honest, my notes reflect a woman who might want to change the big things about herself as well as the small."

"They do? Like what?"

"Like maybe your original purpose no longer fits you. Over the long years, you've changed, but I think you want to change more." I stroke my finger over her downy cheek. She's so sweet. So feral. "At the beginning, you were a mindless force of revenge. Are you that, now?"

"No. I don't think so." She raises her three eyes to mine. "But that's what's so scary."

"That's what's so scary," I agree. "Growing up. Becoming who you want to be, not who someone else tells you that you must be. The hardest thing in the world is to get rid of what no longer serves us and grab onto what does. But I believe in you," I repeat. "You'll find who you want to be, and the world will be better for it, because you're good. In here." I brush over her heart again.

"I am?"

I nod, before I gesture out past the rocky outcrop to the vast vista that is the Sea of Elicher and the distant horizon. "Maybe you'll stay here. Maybe you'll go elsewhere. There's a whole wide world for you to conquer, my perfect Winter Witch."

"Perfect." She huffs air through her nose before reaching for another tissue. After dabbing her face, she disappears all the tissues before kissing my knees, one after the other. "You make it sound so easy, Nick."

"It isn't. But you're incredibly strong. Inside." I pause before I tell her what I've been thinking this last week. "Upon knowing you better and understanding your origins, I'm doubting my original diagnosis. Yes, you exhibit OCD tendencies, but you also exhibit atypical progress. As you've said, you were born to right the world. There's no 'cure' for me to lead you to, but there are techniques I can teach you, so the little upsets don't take away from your joy."

"I feel joy right now," she admits. "I feel... lighter."

"And that makes me happy, because the woman I've come to know deserves nothing less than... bliss."

When my hand lands on her sun-warmed hair, I stroke some strands back behind her ear. In response, she turns into my touch like a cat seeking a caress.

"I have a thought."

"Which is?" She kisses my palm.

"Less thought than potential suggestion."

This time, she smiles. "I'm done with my snit. I'm not going to kill you."

"Promises, promises." I take a deep breath. "You were born to punish those who do wrong. That's your essence, and you're right. It's not my place to tamper with it, nor would I want to. You're magick, and perfect as you are. But there are serious wrongs in this world, wrongs far more horrible than fence posts out of alignment or a disarray of books. Maybe you could choose one or two issues you care about most and narrow your focus upon them rather than trying to right the entire country. You'd still be you, only..."

"Refined." She bends and kisses my knees again before looking up, her expression considering. "I can pick and choose, is what you're saying. I don't need to straighten every chimney, which, to tell the truth, has become pretty boring. I can make my demons pick up litter that blights my perfect land, or punish those who hurt children in vile, deplorable ways."

"For example. Yes."

Though I'm not sure I want to know how she'll punish them. Still, I have to accept the scary, violent parts of who she is. Her essence, as she's said, won't ever change. Better she exhausts her rage on the worst crimes against humanity, even if the justice system objects.

She nods and sniffs. "Okay."

"You're remarkable." And I mean it.

Her fingers trace patterns on my leg as her gaze drops. "I think you're remarkable too, Nick." She takes another staggered breath before she looks up again. "I guess I'm cured."

I start laughing because she looks crestfallen rather than delighted. "Not nearly, but you've made great strides."

Great strides, while I've fallen. It's time for someone else to take over my job. She's ready to work with a real professional who doesn't want to fuck her so badly that his opinions, techniques, and analysis have been compromised.

"Good. You'll stay." She hunkers back on her heels and smiles.

"I said I would. But the therapy part of our relationship should probably end. Soon. I'll recommend some psychologists in Oslo. Let's say we give our sessions another few weeks, though, just to be certain." Because I don't want to leave and need an excuse to stay. "Besides, you haven't finished teaching me to be organized."

She sobers immediately. "That's true." Pausing, her brows draw down but her third eye springs wide as she appears to search her own emotions. "I don't think I want you to worry over unaligned edges like I do. I like you the way you are, Nick. You're perfect, too."

There are no words to describe how my insides roll, melt, and harden as I attempt to reshape to her expectations. A caverning fear fills me that I won't meet them.

I guess I understand her better than I thought. I'm afraid of losing myself, too. In her. But I'm more afraid that I won't measure up to who she needs me to be once I step off the kingly perch of my purpose.

Talk about turning tables.

CHAPTER THIRTEEN:

Lussi

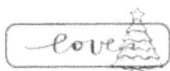

Two days later, I awake to six of my demon horde bouncing on my bed. Though they're careful not to land on me, they seem to consider Nick's hump beneath the covers an incitement to violence.

"Get off me!" He kicks out, but the demons just laugh and continue their childish acrobatics. The others rim the room like sentinels, egging on their companions.

"Can't take the heat, get the hell out of Hell," Rocco snaps, jumping high. I spot his intent to cave in Nick's stomach, and arrest him in midair.

"Get off. All of you." I swish my fingers. The bouncing demons fly to the ground, landing in a messy heap. I pile them like a pyramid instead. Better.

Their wails ring around the room, mixing with their complaints as they claim injury. I swear. If I didn't need them to ride next December 13th, I'd send them all down a deep well.

Sami steps through the doorway, clearing his throat. My manservant appears unusually calm. He's generally the first one to fall atwitter in the midst of a crisis. "My lady, we've come to warn you. There have been some complaints made. Minor matter, of course, but it's um, well, come to the attention of the king's minister that you have a human living below shell, which, as you know, is against the rules."

"It is?" If so, no one ever told me. Which leads to my next point. "Why didn't you tell me there were complaints?"

Sami shrugs. "Your boy-toy was already here, so I figured you didn't care." A red flush covers his face. "You've always held Lucifer's favor."

Beside me, Nick clenches.

"Not in that way," I assure him, though a tiny trickle of happiness flits through me at the thought he might be jealous. Shaking my head, I return my attention to Sami. "Lucifer is no longer in Hell. Any understanding we might have shared is no longer relevant, I suppose." With a full-of-himself archangel on the throne, no one is silly enough to think matters haven't changed, though I've assumed, living on the edge of civilization as I do, I'm safe from notice.

Plus, how was I to know I wasn't allowed visitors? Lucifer certainly never said so. Good thing the orphanage is above shell. I considered at one point relocating it for easier access.

Sami clears his throat before sidling up beside me. Leaning over, he whispers in my ear, "There are those in your horde who feel as if you should have turned to them first to sate your sexual desires." His hands come up in a defensive posture as he backs up a step at my glare. "Just advising you on how matters stand."

Casting Nick a quick glance, I note he's heard it all. His complexion is tomato red, and fire burns in his eyes. It's quite sexy, really, the way he grits his teeth and looks daggers around the room at the demons.

Yup. Definitely jealous.

For his sake, I pitch my response louder than necessary. "I haven't had sex with any of my horde in well over a hundred years. They have no claim on my affections."

Why bother with demons when I have my trusty gadgets? Plus, most of their Kind enjoy a heaping portion of pain with their pleasure, which I'm not into. Though, to be fair, the incubi are fun, at least in the moment. They'll do anything to please a lady, but they leave their lovers with an energy-drained headache the following morning.

"But you might have chosen them, is the point," Sami responds, dropping any pretense of keeping Nick out of the conversation.

I reach up and drag Sami closer by his hair, ignoring the way he begins to glow with arousal under the painful tug. Demons. They're unmanageable. "Take care of this."

"Of course, my lady," he squeaks as he futilely tries to nod. "Only, the minister has dispatched a note. Here." With trembling fingers, he drags it from his pocket.

Snatching it quickly, I release him, and rip open the missive.

Not good. Amidst all the flowery court language, the order is clear: get rid of Nick. Today. Or face worse than the fine outlined in precise handwriting. I'm not worried about the hecates of gold I'll have to pay. I've got plenty. But Nick... they'll execute him.

When I turn my head, my lips almost brush Nick's cheek, he's leaning so close. He's reading the note over my shoulder, conveniently written in English as if the Clerk of Court knew my houseguest would sneak a peek. Nick's expression is grim, and when he finishes, he sighs.

"I suppose I was meant to read this."

I nod. It wouldn't be Hell without layers of intrigue in even the simplest gesture. "No doubt so you can't claim you didn't know when they come to arrest you."

He pales. "And you?"

I don't need to tell him. He reads it on my face.

Helpfully, Sami speaks up. "They'll send her to the Punishing, probably, along with depleting some of her fortune. Everyone knows the new king is mean. The torture she'll experience will be far worse than death."

"Thanks for being so helpful, Sami," I mutter.

Nick's face loosens. He strokes my cheekbone with his thumb. "That's it, then."

"No." I shake my head. "No, I..."

Gently, he draws those long fingers through my hair, his thumb gliding along my cheek again as he interrupts. "You can't think so little of me that you'd imagine I could send you to be tortured. I can't, Luss. I won't."

"You're my prisoner," I say quickly, hating the goodbye I see in his eyes.

"Houseguest. And it appears I've overstayed my welcome." Bending, he grazes my lips with a scorching kiss. Before I can deepen it, he slips from the bed. The pajama pants he wears are tented at the front.

We've been sharing a bed and cuddling, but except for some superficial kisses and the foot massage, nothing untoward has passed between us. Nick wanted to be "professional." I thought we'd have time after the professional ended to explore and learn each other physically, even though the flames have long passed from flickering to outright conflagration. I haven't pressed him because I wanted him to feel comfortable that he wasn't taking advantage of me as his patient.

And now it's too late?

He walks to the closet and starts to withdraw clothing before stopping, shoulders hunched. He gathers himself together, whips a sweatshirt out the closet, and closes the door. After slipping it over his head, hiding the array of chiseled muscles one row at a time, he looks at me.

"My computer?"

I nod towards the dresser. "Bottom drawer. Your phone's there, too." I keep placing his things in different spots, waiting for him to approve one enough so he stops leaving his electronics spread across the space.

A wave of sorrow washes through me. None of his things will ever mess up my home again.

With a flicker of my fingers, I change his pajama pants to jeans. He sends me a small smile and nod of thanks.

When he's packed his few possessions, he gazes around the room as if taking notes for his memory. His eyes fall upon me. "Luss. I..." But his voice is so thick with emotion, he has to clear his throat twice before he can continue. "Thank you. For everything. I wish…"

"What?" I'm across the floor and standing in front of him, my hands wrapped together so they won't do something stupid like cling to him.

He shakes his head. Sighs. Looks to the ground and back at me as he hefts the computer bag strap over his shoulder. "Can we write? Email?"

"Sure." But my chest deflates, the momentary hope that he was somehow offering more evaporating and leaving me mired in deeper despair. Is that it, then? A handful of weeks below shell, which is a lot less time above, enormous changes to my world and to me, and he's gone?

"Maybe we can continue our sessions over video call?"

He sounds so hopeful, I force a smile and say, "Okay."

A relieved expression crosses his face. His cheeks have hollowed during his sojourn with me. He's grown more beautiful. It's a by-product of Hell. When he returns to his world, all the women will be bleeding to get close to him. Maybe they already were.

Before me. After me. All of time without me.

I can't breathe. Someone has scooped out my entire chest, including my lungs.

"Luss." He wants to say more. I can see it—feel it—because so do I, but instead, he just nods.

And I have to send him away before my heart, already on the floor, crushes into a million little pieces. "Goodbye, Nick."

And before he can respond, I swish my fingers and wave him away, not to his hotel room in Norway, but to his mother's home in Connecticut. I've seen it in the photos he's shown me. If I can picture it, I can magick it. Once again, my talent doesn't desert me. It's the only thing I've ever been able to rely upon.

And it's not enough. I'd give it all up to make him stay. I sink to the floor.

I don't think I can get back up.

***

"Good morning." I paste on a bright smile for the camera. Through it, Nick looks fuzzy, like a watercolor running from its edges. But some aspects of him are so ingrained in my mind, I can see them clearly: his mussy hair, his sharp cheekbones—and aren't they more cut than usual?

I'm probably just looking for some sign he's missed me and imagining he hasn't been eating.

Three weeks and two days have passed below shell. According to the calendar, a week has passed above; time never runs in any organized fashion between the two realms.

"Luss. Hi. Is everything okay? It's nearly midnight here."

Oh. "Time runs differently, and I can never pinpoint it exactly, though I have an internal alarm for *Lussi Langnatt*. Comes in handy."

"Guess tha t explains why it was summer below shell and winter above when I was there."

I wait for him to say more, but he glances away before looking back. A strange, strained silence falls between us, mirroring the tone of the emails we've exchanged. I sent the first one only an hour after I sent him to Connecticut. After hounding Sami to make the infernal computer work, I typed out an upbeat greeting with two fingers. I erased more lines than I left standing. It took Nick a full above-shell day to respond. I continue to send him emails every day. He must receive at least three every twenty-four hours.

His responses have been... short. As if now that he's away from me, he'd be happier to never interact with me again, which opens up a cavern inside me I don't think I can ever fill. I've had a lot of pain in my life, but Nick's rejection cuts deeper than anything I could ever imagine.

He glances at his wrist, checking the time on his father's watch that he kept in his computer bag while below shell. Maybe

I'm keeping him from some appointment. Or a date.

At midnight.

The thought brings shivers to my stomach and makes it turn over. Does he have someone there with him? In bed with him?

"Er," I begin, searching desperately for something to add. All the questions I had in my mind, all the discussions I planned, have disappeared like breath upon a mirror.

"How have you been?" His upbeat tone is so false, it makes me cringe.

"Good. Good. And you?"

"Great. Really great. I, um, well, I wrote you. About opening my office for some emergency sessions? And, well, it's kept me busy. Idle hands, devil's playground, and whatnot." His voice stumbles off, and he glances at his watch again.

I can't take this. The conversation is so stilted, I have to sniff back tears. I've missed him so much. The easy camaraderie we developed led me to think he would always be, at the very least, my friend. But all I hear now is the voice of someone who wants to be gone.

Anger, sharp and hot, flares through my veins. I welcome the burn. Better it than the hollow, empty, aching loss that's weighted my limbs and pressed boulders against my chest. "Am I keeping you from an appointment?"

"No! No- just, um, well, there is something I'd like to discuss, but..."

All my antennae are up and waving wildly. I examine his distorted image for some clue as to what he's hiding. But when my gaze travels beyond him to the door, I see the shape of a suitcase, one of those hard cases on wheels. And over the suitcase is his laptop bag and heavy black coat. The outerwear slips down farther on one side and pools on the floor.

He's going somewhere. And he doesn't want me to know. There's only one explanation that makes sense for why he wouldn't have told me about his travel in one of our emails. Why he's stuttering, now. Another woman. No—not another woman. A woman. I'm not in his life at all.

The knowledge slithers into my soul and takes root as I finally acknowledge what my brain keeps trying to tell me: I was a distraction, a fling, and maybe even someone he never wanted to be with at all. I was a danger to be avoided, and having avoided me, he now wants to cut all ties.

The welling of tears behind my eyes is so sharp, I can't continue the conversation. I'm about to try to make excuses to let him go when his eyes widen and he leans in close to the monitor's lens, so close all I can see is one hazel eye and part of his cheek.

When he sits back, his face has firmed. He's not avoiding my gaze any longer. "Who the fuck is that?" He's staring at something past my shoulder.

Confused, I turn around to find an incubus leaning against the doorframe, exuding sexual energy. To the side, just out of camera view, Sami is gesturing wildly.

"I brought you a present," Sami hisses in a low voice.

Despite my anger and my hurt, a sudden burst of panic consumes me. The incubus is tall, dark, and deadly handsome. He's also shirtless. His trousers sit low on his hips, and the button at the waist has popped open, revealing the unmistakable swell of penis head poking out the top. Maybe Nick can't see it.

Yeah. Sure. Maybe he's gone blind.

CHAPTER FOURTEEN:

Lussi

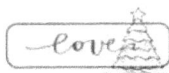

I turn back to the monitor and lock gazes with a pair of narrowed, focused eyes. So. Not blind, then. With a wave of my fingers, I send my helpful servant and his "present" to the middle of the Murgrove swamp. A string of curses fills my head as I stare at Nick, who's glaring at me over the airwaves.

"It's not what you think."

"I think I should have known better." Nick's tone drips acid as his mouth purses like he's sucked a bowl of lemons.

As if he has a right to judge me, when he's about to run off with some woman!

"Maybe you should have," I snap back. I jut my chin towards the suitcase. "Going somewhere?" I demand, my tone sugar sweet.

He turns in a mirror of the action I just performed to see what I'm gesturing to. Even through the foggy lens, I can see him pale. But when he turns back, he squinches his eyes and sighs. "I can't believe I'm such an idiot."

"A brighter man would have set his suitcases out of eyesight when answering a video chat, especially when he's about to go live with some other woman," I agree.

"Not that." His beautiful hazel eyes pop open. "Well... maybe that, but not the other woman part." He waves behind him. "You know what, Luss? I booked a plane that leaves in a few hours. And do you know where I intended to go?"

How can I know, without knowing what woman has her claws into him?

"I was going to Norway. To Oslo. Back to Mundal, to the hotel where we met. I thought I'd surprise you in the hopes you could arrange a few hours above shell." A groan cuts off his words, and he shakes his head. "I'm such a fucking fool."

It takes me a few moments to comprehend his words. We sit in silence, staring at each other, until finally, I'm able to respond. "You were going to come here?"

He nods, an abrupt motion of his head.

And everything in me melts into a puddle. Tears begin streaming down my face. Those falling from the eye on my forehead trail over my nose and plop down to my chest, wetting one of the tee shirts he left behind. I've been wearing it for weeks.

"That man—the incubus—I didn't call for him. Nothing happened, Nick. It was just Sami trying to lift my spirits. I've missed you so much, I've barely left my room in three and a half weeks. I've been moping about until everyone is tired of it, but all I could think was that I had to wait at least a week of your time to video call you. And I've been yelling at the horde, sending them to the Punishing for no reason. But... nothing happened, Nick."

As I speak, his features relax. He inhales a long breath before his lips tilt into a smile. "Do you mean we're both so insecure we think the other had some assignation planned?"

I smile too. "I guess so."

Silence again as we stare. I swipe at my tears.

"I can still make my plane, Luss. If you can spend some time with me above shell, I'd love to visit with you."

"I can spend time above shell." I inhale and twist my fingers. Winds rush as I travel through the ethers. From behind Nick's back, I whisper, "But you don't need to go to Norway to see me. I can visit you."

He rises and turns so suddenly, his chair shoots across the room as if on greased wheels. Neither of us watches it move, having eyes only for each other.

In the next instant, I'm in his arms, all his strong muscles holding me tight as one hand wraps the back of my head and holds me steady. With a hunger I appreciate and return, he devours my lips, my tongue, my mouth, my soul. All I can do is melt into him and try to appease my own need.

With a groan, he rips his lips away. His thumbs move along my cheekbones as I cling to his arms. "Lussi. Are you real? Am I dreaming?"

"I could send a vision, it's true, but I'm really here. As real as you are, anyway." I allow my fingers to trace the curves and divots of his chest under his soft sweater. It's a deep blue color and lends an interesting shade to his eyes. Under my palms, his heart beats fast and strong. It beats for me, I hope. "Surprise?"

"The very best one I could ever imagine," he affirms before stepping back.

The loss of him under my hands hurts, but only for a moment as he draws me to the messy bed in the corner of the room. Seating me gently on the edge, as if I'm made of glass, he sinks to his knees beside me. With tentative hands, he strokes the contours of my legs. They're bare under my skirt. I hadn't thought to change.

But his caresses grow more certain as I don't object. His hands trace the curves of my calves, over my knees, and up my thighs. His thumbs trace perilously close to the spot growing wet under his regard.

"I'm not your therapist anymore, Luss." His voice is deeper than usual and grave, with an intensity that's mirrored in the way he watches me.

"I know. I've hired Mrs. Olstad, like you suggested."

"And you like her?"

"I do. She's not you, but she's kind. She doesn't shrink away from my third eye."

His brow lifts as he smiles. "Is that a joke?"

When I understand what he means, I laugh. *Shrink* away. "Not intentional." I pause. "I've missed you so much, Nick. Except for my two therapy sessions, I've barely gotten out of bed."

His smile grows wicked edges as his thumbs press closer to where I want them. "Bed is exactly where I want you, Luss. There's nothing holding me back from you now." The rest of his fingers splay over my hips, his wide hands engulfing my smaller frame and sending a pounding heat to my core. "I want you. I want to devour you whole and fuck you so you can't stand for days. I want to melt you into a puddle. All you need to do is say yes."

His words are like fire over my skin. They burn and consume all the sensible parts of me, not that I ever intended to resist him. In fact, I intended to seduce him, and it's the disparity between the battle I thought I would have to wage and the turnabout of my conquering hero that makes me too unsteady to respond.

When I don't say yes, his hands still, and he groans. I wiggle, and he moves his palms up under his shirt that I still wear, across my abdomen, and beneath my breasts. A moan of longing leaves my lips as he holds there.

I want him on my nipples. They're hard and aching, just like the rest of me, needing this man, this human, like I've never needed anyone before. From the moment we met, an invisible rope has bound us together.

All that remains is to bind our bodies. I grab his hands and try to move them up, but, unless I use my magick, he's stronger than I am. He refuses to move, waiting for my verbal permission.

"Nick!"

"Tell me, Lussi. Tell me yes. I need the words." He leans in and kisses over where my belly button would be if I had one. Not having been born, I never needed a connection to a mother, but the sudden thought that I'm different, markedly different, makes me still. Of course, he notices my discomfort immediately. "What's wrong?"

"Nothing. I just... I'm not exactly like a human woman, Nick."

His gaze is so penetrating, I feel it down to my core. "What are you telling me,

Luss? That you don't have a pus- er, vagina?"

My hands fly to my mouth, and I shake my head, but he immediately misinterprets, so I have to jolt out, "No! I mean, yes. Yes, I have a... vagina."

"But...?"

"But not a belly button." I rush the words to get them out of my mouth.

He repeats them slowly before merriment flashes across his features. "That's okay. I've never fucked a belly button, and I've no desire to start now. So long as you have a sweet pussy I can pet and lick and make love to, we're good."

I feel the heat on my cheeks at his words. I don't know why. I've had lovers. They've called my parts all sorts of things, and I've never minded. But the way he purrs the word "pussy" makes me think of a little kitten rubbing up against him, seeking his caresses. Seeking his praise. The word out of his mouth is sin and luxury.

"Say yes, Lussi, because I need to do more than hold you like this." He leans in again and presses kisses along my abdomen. "Say yes."

So I do, because all I want is to feel him inside me. He's big and strong, like a Viking, but soft and gentle, like the best incubi. And I need him, too. "Yes. Fuck me, Nicholas Frye. But make it good."

My little joke causes him to nip at the soft rounds of my belly. "Bad girl. I'll give the orders in bed if you don't mind."

The fleeting discomfort of his teeth fades quickly. His words hang in my ears and on my skin. "I don't mind," I whisper.

I don't mind so much that I'm streaming like a waterfall between my legs.

"Good girl," he growls, earning a mewl from me in response and another gush.

I feel his smile against my skin as he begins to press kisses around my breasts. The sides. Above. In the hollow between the two rounds. Everywhere I don't need him. His head disappears beneath the shirt.

So I wave our clothing away.

He laughs against my skin, sending little trills of fire through me. "Convenient."

His hands stroke over my arms, whisper light caresses that leave me mewling again and arching up as he brings his lips near my pebbled nipples.

He moans in appreciation, his hands moving to weigh my breasts in his palms. Finally. Those skilled thumbs move over the hard pink nubs in circles, making them ache into my core and finally, *finally*, he leans and sucks one onto his tongue.

And I see stars. Nothing in my entire fifteen hundred years has felt so perfect. His mouth is hot against my cooler skin, warming me to the depths of my soul.

As strands of lightning fling through my veins, I press him closer. He doesn't disappoint, sucking on me as if he would drag me into him, but then he moves to the other peak, and I die a little more. Nothing can feel this good and be right. But if it's wrong, I don't care.

With a long groan that pierces me to my depths, he rips his mouth away to feather open kisses across my cheek, down my throat, across the bones of my shoulder, and even into the inner space of my elbow. And all the while, his hands are moving in circles over my skin, lighting starlight and sunbursts until I'm just a mewling, helpless mess of sensation and awe.

My lids flutter closed as I lay back on the messy bed, and for the first time in my long life, I'm glad it's not perfect. I want mess. I want chaos. I want not to know where he's going to land or fly to next.

He pushes me up and adjusts his body between my legs. I'm delirious with hunger. With need. I'm a gaping hole waiting to be filled, an empty vessel into which I need him to pour himself.

"Fuck, Lussi, you're so gorgeous. You're so damned perfect." He whispers the words against my skin after he gazes down my smooth belly and groans. "And your pussy." With resolute fingers, he pulls apart my thighs.

"Yes, Nick, yes." Just in case there's any confusion.

The play of light and shadow over his rippled expanse captures my attention. Behind his slender, Viking form lies a brain more capable and strong than his muscles, but it's his body that delights me now.

As I reach for him, he lowers his head between my legs, inhaling deep before growling in response.

In the next moment, his mouth is against my skin, parting my folds with his tongue. He snakes through the valley and suckles at my passage. I writhe a little to try to tempt him toward my clit, but when he stabs his tongue into my heat, I forget about the need to have him suckle in favor of having him torture me further with the tensile appendage.

Air escapes me as a whine. I gulp as my limbs begin to tremble, but I can't inhale. My body starts to shake, and my legs collapse. Nick pushes them to each side, giving him further room to taste me.

"Don't you dare come, Lussi," he growls, the words vibrating against my most sensitive flesh. "Not yet."

But my body is already winding into a tight corkscrew. My sight is blackening at the edges. I can no more stop the freight train speeding down the tracks than I can...

"Lussi." He flicks his fingers against my inner thigh to get my attention, but the only thing it does is hurtle me over the precipice. I burst like fireworks and dissipate at my edges.

When I land back on earth, he's kissing up my stomach again, grinning.

"Don't laugh," I croak, tugging on his mussy hair. "I've waited a long time for you to do that."

He lands his lips against mine. "I made you come without even touching your clit. I get bonus points, darling."

Darling. I'm distracted by the term. I'm someone's *darling.* Me. The Winter Witch of Norway.

I lock my lips to his one more time before flopping my head back onto the bed. "And what will you do with those bonus points?"

"Make you give me a boon, I think."

"A boon? What kind of boon?" Anything. Anything he wants.

He kisses my lips again, this time deepening the embrace. I taste myself on him, and it reminds me how much I want to taste all of him. I reach down and grab his cock.

He startles up and then laughs. "Fuck, I think I love you."

And we both still, boon forgotten, or at least, postponed.

CHAPTER FIFTEEN:

Nick

love

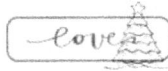

I don't know how those words slipped out. It's too soon. We've only known each a couple of months, not that I can do the math with any degree of accuracy, what with above shell and below shell time running so differently.

I should take back my words. Pretend I love her magick or something.

"It's true. I love you." The absence of prevarication just spills out of my mouth.

Maybe my tongue knows better than my brain does.

The time we've spent apart has been awful. I've pawned off my clients on other therapists just to go back to Norway for the potential of a few hours together. When a man is willing to fly across the globe to spend minutes with a woman, he should probably admit that he's in so deep, the sky is just something he's heard about.

I lean on one arm and use the other to smooth the white and silver hair from Lussi's third eye; it's staring at me without blinking. "Living without you has been impossibly hard. I don't want to pressure you. It's okay if you don't…"

"I love you too, Nick," she interrupts. "I love you so much, you're an agony in my chest and between my thighs, a missing I can't seem to fill without touching you." She bites her full bottom lip in invitation.

Swooping, I replace her teeth with my own. I bite just hard enough to draw a tiny spot of blood that I taste with my tongue. "I'm not always gentle," I say, baring my heart. "Sometimes, I like it rough. I'll try to temper my urges for you..."

"I don't want temperance."

"But if you're uncomfortable..."

"I'll swat you over the head. I don't like pain."

"That was as much as I'd ever want to hurt you..."

"But being rode hard is totally in my wheelhouse." I start to smile at the expression, but the urge leaves me when she says, "Fuck me, Nick. Fuck me hard."

What's a guy to do?

She wraps her legs around my waist, arching close to my dick. Those amazing stomach muscles allow her to draw her pussy up to where I hover. One swipe, and I'm done.

Fuck. I'm going to come before I ever get inside her. I run my dick through her folds, gathering her wetness, before centering. With a slight tilt of my hips and a groan on my lips, I press.

She feels like heaven around me. She's so slick with arousal, I can slide the head right in, but her tight walls keep me from going any further.

"Nick!"

Hot softness clamps around the tip of my raging dick. My balls tighten, and my seed begins to spiral up my shaft. Going up on one elbow, I grip the base to try to contain my impending orgasm.

It's too late. Not even halfway inside her, I explode like some adolescent with his first girlie magazine. Hot spurts of seed rip from my body so fast and hard, I can't even withdraw from her perfect, tight embrace before I come.

When I can catch my breath, I pull out and collapse next to her, mortified. "Luss, I'm sorry."

"Ri..." She can't finish for laughing. Great. Just what a guy wants to hear. My fucking cum is spilling from her, and she's in hysterics.

When she finally calms, still smiling wide, she asks, "Do I get bonus points, too?"

"Witch."

She leans up on one elbow to brush her lips against mine. "I didn't use magick."

"You used you, which is enthralling enough." Her hair falls over her third eye, so I stroke it behind her ear, only to have it drop again. "I love you so much, Lussi. I'm sorry. I wanted our first time to be, well, magical."

"It was, actually. Nothing like a little premature ejaculation to tell a girl she's wanted."

"In that case, you should know I'm regularly on the verge of coming just thinking about you. I don't even need you to be touching me. Though I'd prefer it."

Her eyes sparkle with delight as she brushes her lips against mine. Her nipples swish over my chest, and just like that, just like I'm a teenager again with a constant hard-on, my dick jumps.

"Ooh, is someone seeking redemption?"

I bring the back of my hand to my forehead. Fucking dick. "Desperately."

But when she slides down my body, she surprises me by wrapping her lips around the head. Gently, softly, she sucks me over her tongue, and the biggest shock is how I jolt into full length once more.

"Yummy." She pops her lips off me. I miss her heat before she slides her lips around me once more.

Everything in me spirals up again at her tentative but certain movements. She's clearly taking note of what I like, which is everything she does, but when she presses her tongue hard against the vein along the underside of my shaft, I can't help the strangled sounds of pleasure that leave me.

And then she deep-throats me. A rage of fire ants crawls up my spine and twinkles through my blood. My hands want to hold her in place and stop her from retracting, but I force them away from her head. She's delicate and sweet. I don't want to hurt her.

But I want to ram myself so far down, I find her pussy from the wrong end.

As if she knows what I'm thinking, she draws back to the tip and then plunges. Hard. I push so deep that my balls brush her lips. I can't hold back. My seed spurts long and hot until my legs are left shaking and the base of my spine curls around emptiness.

She slithers up my body, and I manage to wrap her in my arms. When she cuddles into my chest with a happy snuffling sound, clearly pleased with herself, I smile.

"I have no idea how that happened again. You've... you're so incredible."

"Not bad yourself, Nicky." She pats my chest before her mouth rounds into a yawn. "Sorry. I haven't been sleeping well since you left."

"Me, too." But I run the last few minutes through my mind again before chuckling. "Is there anything you're not perfect at?"

Tapping her chin, she pretends to consider before laughing, too. "Guess not."

"Modest, too. When I get my strength back, I'm giving you three extra orgasms. No arguing."

"Would I argue with you?" She laughs again and kisses my chest.

"Constantly, which is only one of the things I love about you. Have I mentioned in the last three seconds how much I adore you?" I kiss the top of her head, barely able to muster the energy to lean up to do so before flopping back down.

"Not nearly enough." A wider yawn stops her words. She snuggles closer.

"Blanket," I mumble, attempting to sit up to retrieve the cover lying folded at the foot of the bed.

She flicks her fingers. It envelopes us both.

And as I drift into sleep, her skin pressed to mine once more, I smile at how right it feels to be holding her. Finally.

CHAPTER SIXTEEN:

Lussi

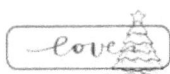

When I awake the next morning, alone, I'm unclear where I am. The room has pale blue walls and some sort of hideous modern printed rug on the floor. A series of weights rests in one corner. On the opposite end, a table with a bunch of electronics takes up a large piece of the wall. A laptop is open and facing the door where a suitcase stands.

My sleep-fogged mind slowly clears. Nick's room. It's messy, but far more ordered than I would have credited, as if he's tried to keep my lessons in mind.

Just as I've tried to learn his.

The memories rush in, filling me with such enormous joy, I don't know how to contain or process it. I try to hold in my emotions for fear they'll escape, but there's no denying how happy I am to be in Nick's bed. In Nick's bedroom. In Nick's life.

He loves me. He loves me—The Winter Witch of Norway. The fact is unfathomable, and yet, I trust him not to lie about something so important.

From across the apartment, the sound of dishes clattering and male cursing floats to my ears. Slipping on one of the tee-shirts I find scrunched on top of his dresser (a little touch of disorder I find enchanting, because it's his), I give the room a quick magickal straightening before going in search of Nick.

There's a long, narrow hall. To my right is a living room, and at the far end is a marble counter behind which a kitchen opens. Steam billows from the sink as my boyfriend runs the cold water over something hot.

Boyfriend? Manfriend? Lover? I don't know the acceptable term for what he is to me now, but it's on my agenda today to find out.

"Smells delicious." It smells like burnt garbage, but his abashed expression when he rotates means I'll sample whatever he's cooked simply to please him.

"Do I get points for having tried to make you breakfast?" His eyes dart everywhere, from my fluffy hair to my naked legs and feet extending from the bottom of his shirt.

I slide onto one of the stools on the opposite side of the marble expanse. "I like this points system, but you should know I'm competitive."

He shakes his finger at me before flipping it and gesturing me closer. "Nope. Not there. Here. Now." His eyes point the way next to him.

There's a gentleness in his command and a twinkle in his disorderly eyes that tells me I'll want to obey. "Orders? When you've burnt my breakfast?"

His lips quirk as an evil look falls over his hewn features. "Orders if you want to earn a 'good girl.'"

"Tyrant."

"Witch."

I slide off my stool and skirt the counter until I stand toe to toe with him. He wraps me in his arms, his fingers winding into the hair on the back of my head, and brushes a soft kiss across my lips. "Good morning, darling," he growls in the way that has me rushing like a river between my legs.

"Good morning, Nick." I pop up onto my toes and circle my arms around his neck, before pulling him down for a deeper kiss. He tastes like the coffee cooling in the cup behind him. Delicious.

Another growl becomes a groan as he does his pulling-my-soul-through-his-lips thing. My entire body is quivering by the time he pulls back. "Yes."

"Yes, what?"

"Yes, we're on a points system because otherwise, you're going to try to roll right over me for the rest of my life and I'm going to let you. Which is okay, most of the time, but I'd like a few moments of clear victory." His smile widens, and he rolls his hips so the bulge in his pajama pants squishes against my stomach. "Of course, if you want submission from me, I could give it a try. Now would be a good time to practice."

I rub my hardening nipples against his chest. Even through his tee-shirt, I can feel his ripples of muscles.

"Nope. Forget submission. I need to control this, or I'm going to come too soon again." He grabs me and holds me still.

"Your sex skills are better than your cooking skills."

With a laugh, he lifts me up. My legs circle his waist and he holds my ass to keep me steady. "Bet you say that to all the guys."

His neck is sweet and smells like sleep as I nuzzle against his skin. "Only the ones I love."

He grabs my hair and gently forces my head back so he can look into my eyes. "Just me then?"

"Just you."

"Good." He kisses me again, doing the suck-up-my-soul kiss he must have invented. I've never really liked kissing, but I love kissing him.

He carries me down the hall as if I weigh no more than feathers. This time, he's all business. After tossing me down on the bed, he strips off his pants and follows me to the mattress, his dick already sliding through my folds. He doesn't waste time on preliminaries, and I'm glad. I'm already so ready for him, my body is weeping.

Plunging into me, he goes balls-deep in one stroke. I close around him with a gasp, the burn and stretch tearing all the air from my lungs. He's large and long, and beautifully centered. I want every inch of him.

With a strained expression, he waits without moving for me to relax around him. Attuned to me as no one else has ever been, not even the incubi, whose job it is to know such things, he intuits the moment the burning recedes and my body is ready for more. Crashing his lips against mine, devouring me as if I'm his only means of survival, he slips his hand between our bodies.

Seeking fingers circle my clit, gathering moisture before sliding across my plumping nub. At the same moment he draws his hips back and plunges again. With the second stroke, he finds my G-spot.

Everything in me tenses as he rubs the sensitive flesh. With each stroke of his fingers and dick, he winds me into a quivering mass of need. It's acid and satin, fire and water, and by the time I'm gasping for air, he's growling my name as his balls tighten against my folds.

With an explosion that tears me from my body, I come around him—so long that even the stars fall from the sky. I'm distantly aware that he shouts his own release.

When he collapses next to me, still inside me, I'm blissed out on love. I want nothing more than to lie cuddled with him inside me forever.

Until he screams.

.

CHAPTER SEVENTEEN:

Nick

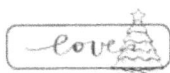

"Damn it!"

Thirty demons, recognizable by their horrific above-shell features, tumble through the doorway, snickering and pointing at my flaccid cock as it slips from Lussi's hot passage.

"Get the fuck out of here!" I try to jump to my feet with the mad intention of laying them flat, the whole ugly, horrific bunch of them, but Lussi holds me with her magick. "Damn it, let me go!"

She pulls the sheet off the bed and wraps it around her body. "Not until you calm down. You can't take on demons, Nick."

"Fuck yes, I can. Watch me." But my arms are held down at my side, and my feet don't move. "Stop holding me. How are they here? Why are they here?"

"Well, as I think I mentioned, demons can travel above shell in their own bodies, but those bodies twist to reveal the true nature of their souls. Lucifer's rules. Their spirits can also inhabit humans on occasion. Tougher to see. As to the why…" She rotates back to the group. "I'm sure you don't have a pass, and you're not supposed to be above shell without me."

"Which we are. With you." One of them steps forward, bows to Lussi, then points at my shriveled dick and laughs. "Hope that thing grows!"

I'm definitely killing him first. He has a horse's head cleaved through the middle, an eyeball rolling down his cheek, warts up and down his body, and an erect, naked cock made of what looks to be red brimstone. Plus, there's a series of spikes where his forehead should be.

"Resting state, Bozzo. Or maybe you don't know about that because you never get laid?" Luckily, no one froze my tongue. "Release me, Lussi."

"Not a chance, darling. I love you too much." But she turns and brushes a kiss over my cheek before sighing.

Brimstone-dick wrinkles his snout at me before returning his attention to Lussi. "Er, my lady, we come with a message."

Lussi sighs again. "What is it now, Sami?"

Sami? The nice, helpful manservant who made me picnics and helped me leave partial messes everywhere to trip up Lussi?

"I bring a message from the court, my lady." He bows low, giving me an unfettered glimpse of bone under the gaping cut through his head before he presents her with a rolled scroll.

Sighing again, Lussi accepts the message and wiggles up to a sitting position. The sheet bands her nipples as she presses her arms against her sides to keep it in place. I don't mind at all that she's reserving her beauty solely for my eyes. I mind a lot that I don't get to see it right now because of a rag-tag bunch of demons.

After skimming the message, her face falls. The scroll snaps back into place. "The new chancellor insists I am above shell without permission. He's ordering me back for a meeting with the king to explain why, which is ridiculous. When Lucifer gave me accommodations in Hell, there was an understanding."

"Which was?" I can't move toward her to read the damned scroll for myself. All I can do is turn my head until she releases me from her magick.

"I agreed not to wreak vengeance three-hundred and sixty-four days of the year in exchange for habitation below shell. I never once agreed to remain below shell for the entirety of those days." Her voice snaps. She's clearly unimpressed with the order as she tosses the scroll back to Sami, who scrambles on the floor to retrieve it. "There's my answer, which is a resounding 'no.' Tell Senefer to fuck off, and if he has any further questions, he can go find Lucifer and ask him about it."

"Er, my lady, perhaps King Michael isn't aware of your understanding? Perhaps a meeting with him might be best?"

Fire sparkles and dies across the paper as Lussi points to it. "Now he's advised. Go back to Hell. All of you." She waves her hand, and the horde disappears along with what's left of the flaming scroll.

"Luss?"

"Right. Sorry." After a twist of her finger, she shimmies back against the pillows, trying to get comfortable. But she's still frowning. "Damned nuisance. Lucifer married a human and abandoned Hell. At least he was reasonable, but his brother? Ugh." Her frown deepens, and her gaze skitters away.

Released from my stasis, I scramble to sit up, facing her. "What's going on?"

"It's not important."

Bad sign. "Am I going to have to fight the King of Hell to keep you?"

Her laugh has sad edges and ten tons of disbelief. "Can't fight an archangel, Nick. Even I can't do that." She rubs the sheet over her leg. "Lucifer was serious about day passes. Michael is probably ten times worse. I'm going to have to talk to him, make him see reason, but there's a law about Kinds mating and..."

When her gaze drifts to the far side of the room rather than meeting mine, I feel an awful lot like a betrayed wife who's just realized she knows nothing of the family's finances. "Luss? Are you saying we can't be together?"

She bites her lip and finally, *finally*, looks at me. "I don't know. The laws are... convoluted. But I know I'm not in breach of my visitation rights. I'm like a Tarasque. I was born of a curse above shell and therefore have the absolute right to stay above shell should I choose."

"Great. Then no problem."

She nods. "Right. No problem."

"Except?" My hand skims down her throat, and I press my thumb into the hollow of her neck. Gently. Lightly. I'm not trying to hurt her, which I'd never do, or express dominance, which I'd love to do. I just enjoy feeling the thrum of her pulse beneath my finger.

Her gaze skitters once more before returning. "Except Kinds can't intermarry without express permission from Lucifer, and he rarely grants it. Although..." Her voice trails off. It's clear an idea is fluttering through her brain, and she's examining it.

I press my thumb just the tiniest bit deeper to drag her back to me. "Although?"

She reaches for my hand and brings my thumb to her lips. Biting into the flesh, she erases the sting with a kiss. "Although—I'm getting ahead of myself based upon one fantastic night and morning of sex with you."

"Wait until I've fucked you a few more times. I'll perform better. I'm still too overexcited that I'm able to love you." I'd better perform better, or she'll leave me for some incubus. "What part are you getting ahead of? The marriage part?" Even I can hear my heart thumping like a jungle drum.

A low pink blush spreads over her face, and she shrugs. "It's not really at issue."

"Actually, it is."

Despite everything—the fact she's The Winter Witch of Norway and I'm some unassuming psychologist, the fact she's magick and I can barely trip out of my own way, the fact she's amazing and I'm some shlub with good biceps—I know in my heart this is the right move. I knew it yesterday when I asked my mother for my grandmother's diamond engagement ring in preparation for my flight to Norway.

Jumping from the bed, I cross to my suitcase where it still stands packed beside the door and reach into the side pocket. When I return to the bed, I climb up onto my knees before her.

I'm naked. My flaccid dick is hanging like an unappetizing worm. My breath probably smells like gargoyles and stale coffee. I had other plans involving a lovely dinner with wine and candlelight, but I can't wait any longer.

I snap open the black velvet box and present her with a view of a ring in an old-fashioned setting before I clutch her hand. "Lussi, will you do me the incredible honor of becoming my wife?"

The two-karat, mine-cut diamond holds a trace of gray mystery at its heart. Around it, whiter sparkly diamonds set off the middle stone. In the back of my head, from the moment I met The Winter Witch, I think I had my grandmother's ring in mind.

Lussi's face remains strangely blank. Her third eye narrows before enlarging. I can't interpret what she's thinking.

Fuck that. I squeeze her fingers. "We're meant to be together, Luss. We're fated, like stars and sky."

What I don't expect are tears. They begin pouring down her face like a waterfall released from a dam. My heart stutters and the box drops to the bed, but in the next instant, she's in my arms, pressing kisses against my face, my neck, my chest, everywhere and anywhere she can reach.

"I love you. I love you so much, Nick."

I wrap my hands in her hair and pull her back just enough to run my gaze over her face, searching for her answer. "Is that a yes?"

"Yes! Yes, of course it's a yes." She snatches up the box without looking at it and hands it to me. "Please."

Slipping the circlet onto her fourth finger is the most satisfying accomplishment I've ever managed. I touch the ring. "I love you, Luss. So much. I know I've been a jerk in so many ways, always pushing you to act differently, to delve inside yourself, when my own small realizations had to be pounded into my head. But I can't regret anything that led us to this moment. You're amazing, and I'm so honored you'll agree to go through life with me."

"I'm going to do everything in my power, Nick. Everything."

But after our hugging and kissing descends into another round of fucking, after my dick is nested safe within her warm body, spent and still aching for more because I can't seem to get enough of her, she wraps her leg over my hip and sighs.

"Although we do have a little problem." She twists her hand, examining how the diamonds refract light before meeting my gaze. "Marrying you is against the law."

"Unless?" I pounce on the hesitation.

"Unless we seek out Lucifer and get his express permission."

Seek out Lucifer.

That's not a sentence I ever imagined hearing, let alone something I would contemplate doing. I never even considered the devil was real until Lussi mentioned him.

"I'd be more comfortable," I say carefully, "going to the current king." Because call me crazy, but I'd rather deal with an archangel than the Prince of Darkness.

"I don't know Michael. Luce and I have an established relationship. He's protected me for years, plus, even though he gave away his throne, he's still a controlling and powerful deity. Plus-plus, Michael will almost certainly want his brother's assurances about my ability to live above shell without a pass. Plus-plus-plus, technically, Lucifer is also an archangel."

But an infamous one I'm not anxious to meet. Unless he wants a spot on my couch, I'm out of my element. I want to object to Lussi's choice to seek him out, but I don't know anything about Hell's politics or laws.

She does. Which means, I have to trust her.

"Has Lucifer granted exceptions before?"

"He made one for himself when he married Queen Rose. She's human. And there's talk of negotiations for Leonids who wish to go live above shell since their species is dying out below. Something in the atmosphere, they think. But it's not settled yet."

Apparently, neither are we.

Either king is going to hate me. Probably, they'll join together to skin me alive. If Lucifer, The Devil, The Devil, has protected Lussi as she's said, he's going to want a full accounting from me.

And how's that going to go? *Yes, Sir, I did insist Lussi spend time with me and reveal her inner landscape, but she threatened to kill me, you see, and even though self-preservation quickly stopped being the reason I wanted to be with her, it was one of my reasons at the start, not to mention how I wanted proof of the supernatural. Yes, I'm a sniveling coward not to have simply accepted death. Yes, I'm not worthy of her magnificence or her tender heart. Yes, I shouldn't have tried to change one hair on her precious head. And yes, I broke the most serious of my professional ethical codes. Please don't kill me.*

Of course, he'll despise my tactics. I despise my tactics, though I'm happy where they've landed me.

When I voice my concerns, Lussi laughs and smacks my chest. "Luce won't care about any of that. All he cares about is bravery, and you've got a lot of that, although you do need to stop screaming every time one of my demons pops up. Anyway, I'm the one who showed up in your room last night. I'm the one who kidnapped you to Hell in the first place."

"As your houseguest."

"I'm not sure he'll see it that way." Her features soften as she looks at me. With a quick motion, she turns our bodies so I'm lying beneath before she begins kissing down my chest.

My unruly dick jumps to attention, even though he's just gone through the most mind-blowing sex anyone's ever had. When her hot mouth brushes against my enlarging member, I groan and cover my eyes with the back of my hand.

The Devil is going to have to understand because I refuse to give Lussi up, and not just because of the great sex.

Because I don't want to live without her. Hell, I'll even accept her demons.

Figuratively, and literally.

CHAPTER EIGHTEEN:

Lussi

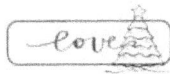

When we step out onto the sand, Nick stumbles, unused to traveling through the ethers. "Careful. Take a moment for balance," I advise.

Heat, hot and desultory, drops upon us like a blanket. I welcome it, but even the breeze over the water fails to cool the sweat that rapidly breaks out over his skin. It's high noon on the equator. It's hotter than Hell.

I magick him a hat. Heat mostly enters and escapes through the head. I love Nick's brains. No sense addling his pate.

"Thanks." He shifts the brimmed straw as he speaks through gritted teeth, searching our environs with wild eyes.

He's probably looking for the best place to vomit, but I'm content taking in the beauty of the green fronts meeting white sand and a blue ocean so profound, it's like a nighttime sky dotted with sapphire streaks. The colors above shell are so much more profound than below.

Nick makes that sound people make before they throw up. Quickly, I touch his face and use my magick to settle his stomach.

He inhales, testing, before smiling. "Thanks, darling. So. Where are we?"

"Tobago. If rumor is correct, Luce is honeymooning here. Come on." I drag Nick up the narrow path that smooths out to paved stones bordered by low stone walls and an array of flowering plants. Everything smells sweet and salty. "I wouldn't mind honeymooning here, too. What do you think?"

"I'm not sure he'll leave me alive for a honeymoon. I think you'll be burying what remains of my body somewhere along this path. He'll leave something to bury, won't he? A finger, maybe, or a toe?"

"Silly." I wrap my hand around his arm and squeeze. "He's a sweetie."

Nick rolls his eyes as if I've lost my mind. He'll see. Just as long as he keeps his cool, he'll be fine, though clearly, he's not looking forward to conversing with Lucifer. This newfound pessimistic streak he's exhibiting is weird, given he's generally an optimist.

Travel is expanding what I know of my fiancé.

Fiancé. I have a fiancé.

Then again, it's true that Lucifer, for all his kindness to me, operates on his own agenda. And he's a stickler for the rules.

"I'm sure he won't appreciate a pop-in," Nick grumbles.

"I'm sure he already knows we're here. Can't turn back now." I squeeze Nick's hand and draw him toward cottage number 18, The Devil's favorite number. If he's still on the island, this will be his room. Before either of us can change our minds, I rap upon the door.

Nick looks like he's going to fade into the white stone at our feet, but he draws himself straighter and edges in front of me as if to protect me from The Devil. It's such a sweet and totally useless gesture, my insides all run together into a melty, gooey puddle.

But when the door opens, a pretty redhead in a pale pink linen sheath stretched over a beachball belly stands there, blinking at us. "Hello?"

I try to push past Nick, but he holds me back. "Hello," he says, though his voice breaks halfway through the word. Clearing his throat, he tries again. "Hello. Are you Rose? We're here to see—um... that is, if your um... is...?"

Rose looks up as if listening before she nods. "He says to come on in."

Nick's face pales to the color of three-day-old fish. I magick away his hat because he's not going to remember to take it off. I don't wish to appear impolite.

Rose stands back and waves us into the cool white plaster cottage. "Go straight through. He's in the suite to the left." A twinkle sparkles across her face. "I can't guarantee his mood because he's trying his hand at the impossible. Meanwhile, I'll take the iced tea out of the refrigerator. It's decaffeinated, unfortunately, but peach infused. Can't have caffeine apparently, not even when carrying the spawn of Satan, which seems abysmally unfair."

"It really does." Most decaffeinated beverages taste like tin and dirt, so I can sympathize.

Dragging Nick through the living room with its white sofa, chairs, and tropical woods, we stop at the door of a bedroom. Curses roll out to greet us. I pull a resisting Nick through the doorway to find Lucifer on his knees, back to us, an array of pale wood stakes spread before him.

He tosses a sheet of white paper. "Fucking ridiculous company. I'm going to burn it to the ground." He doesn't so much stand as twist and emerge from the floor like a growing stalk. "Lussi. And..." His celestial blue eyes land on Nick, who's shaking so hard, he looks like he's being electrocuted. "Nicholas Frye."

I pulse some magick into Nick, just a bit of a calming drought. Otherwise, I think his heart might explode. Lucifer knows exactly what I've done, of course. He knows everything since this is his world.

"Either of you know how to assemble Swedish box store furniture? Rose has her heart set on a crib she found in some catalogue, and she won't let me simply create it. 'Work with your hands, and you'll appreciate fatherhood more,' or some such nonsense. What's a husband to do?"

Nick, still shaking, attempts to pull me behind him. Lucifer raises a brow.

It's better for all of us if I just get to the point. "Sorry to interrupt your honeymoon, Luce, but I need an exception. I want to marry Nick, but he's a human, and your laws, et cetera." I wave my hand as if his laws are piddling things, when even I know they're set in tungsten steel.

Before he can answer, Rose calls from the living room. "I have tea and *cassava pone*. And don't mind my husband, even if he's glowering at you. He's just hangry."

"Hungry and annoyed more than angry, but still excellent timing, Rose." He gestures us toward the living room where his wife is waiting.

I have to push Nick along and practically kick at the back of his knees to get him to sit beside me on one section of the sofa. On the other, Lucifer sinks beside his new bride, sitting so close it's an easy thing for him to lean in and kiss her cheek. The gesture is so unlike the deity I've known for nearly fifteen hundred years, I have to blink.

With a wave of his hands, we each receive a sweating tall glass of iced tea and a plate on which the *cassava pone,* a local cake, apparently, is sliced, forks waiting. To be polite, I lift mine and take a heaping bite.

"Oh, that's good," I sigh after swallowing. The sweetness remains in my mouth. The cake is chewy and moist.

"It's the pumpkin, cassava root, and coconut that give it the gooey yet firm texture, but the tang is from the nutmeg. It's wonderful, right?" Rose lifts her plate and smiles. "We went to Trinidad to walk around yesterday and bought some from a street vendor. I'm hooked. I figure it doesn't matter what I eat since I'm already fat."

"You're not *fat.*" Lucifer spits the word. "You're glowing and so beautiful, you take my breath. And the bump you insult is my child." But he leans in and strokes her long red hair back from her face, and when she tilts her lips up, he kisses them. For a long, long time.

When he finally sighs and sits back against the cushions, his hand on his wife's leg, he looks at me. I can feel him moving through my mind, studying me. I don't need to explain anything. He'll read it from the two of us faster than we'd be able to get the words out.

But when he addresses Nick, I sit very still. There's no way I can fight The

Devil if he comes down on the wrong side of practical.

"Interspecies relationships are forbidden for a variety of reasons, not least because of the changes in the evolution of Kinds when bloodlines mix."

Nick grips his plate as if it's the only thing keeping him alive, and he sits at the end of the piece of furniture, ready to flee. But he leans ever so slightly in front of me. Protecting me.

It takes a bit for him to stutter his response. "I d-don't n-need ch-children. I only w-want L-lussi."

Lucifer smiles. His expression would freeze ice pops. "How very selfish of you. Nick. When you die, Lussi will have to continue her life without you, and without children, too."

"Lucifer." Rose snaps his name before covering his hand with hers.

"These are valid concerns, my love."

"You didn't think twice about them with me."

"What worked for us will not work so well for Nick." But Lucifer looks at me, not Nick, and his dare falls into my head. "What will you give, Lussi? What gifts will you renounce for him?"

And I understand what I should have foreseen as Nick sputters and pales. I squeeze his arm and answer out loud. "Everything. Anything you ask of me." My magick. My immortality. Future children. I don't care about any of it because, for the first time in my life, I'm living. Without the man beside me, there's only the counting of hours as eternity unwinds.

"Are you certain?" he asks in my head. "It's unlike you to be so rash."

"Following your example, Luce."

He huffs before his gaze lands again on Nick. This time, he asks his question out loud. "And you, Nicholas. What will you be willing to give up in order to take Lussi for your bride? You won't have children. That's my unbreakable law, but what else? I'd say your life depends upon your answer, but I'm sure you already know that." Lucifer sends Nick a feral smile, one that makes Nick's bones shake.

But he only leans further in front of me. "Everything. Anything you ask of me," he says, repeating my words and not stuttering in the least.

"Nick, what did we discuss about making promises to supernatural—"

"I don't care, Lussi." He keeps his eyes on The Devil for a long moment before turning his gaze upon me. "But now that he's raised the point... he's right. It's selfish of me to expect... I forgot, in the absolute bliss of knowing you, that I'll not only die, but I'll also age. I don't want you to have to take care of me when I'm a doddering old fool."

"Compared to now when you're a young fool?" I click my tongue at him, still annoyed he was going to promise anything to Lucifer. "I'm not dealing with your second thoughts. They're stupid. But we are going to have a major discussion when we get back home about promising supernatural entities broad scale agreement. I'm thinking about deducting a lot of points from your score."

"Didn't you just promise him anything?" he demands.

"Yes, but... but I'm willing to give anything."

"Well, so am I." Nick glares at me. "Just because I'm not some hotshot witch doesn't mean I can't make a deal with The Devil if I want to. Right?" He sends his glare across the space, and it dies somewhere before Lucifer's scowl.

I'm sure Nick's heart drops to his stomach just as mine does.

"Wait." I hold up my hand to keep The Devil at bay before looking back at Nick. "Come to think of it, I don't like that you're having second thoughts."

"I'm not. Not about loving you. But..."

Nope. Don't want to hear it. "We're getting off track," I interrupt. "I want to take care of you through thick and thin. I'm not just in this relationship for the mind-blowing sex. You need to deal with that."

Rose coughs into her hand. Lucifer chuckles and leans back against the cushions. He's probably enjoying the show.

I reach for Nick's hand and squeeze. "I'm here because you reached into the deepest parts of me and didn't care what you found. You love me, The Winter Witch of Norway. I've killed and decimated, and you still look at me as if I set the stars."

"I'm not sure you didn't." The burning look in his disorderly eyes as he holds my gaze tells me the truth of it: he truly thinks I'm amazing.

"I didn't." I crook my thumb at Lucifer. "He did."

"Not all of them," The Devil responds with false modesty.

I look only at Nick. "It would be my honor to give up immortality and magick for you, Nicholas Frye. Will you take care of me when I'm ancient and doddering?"

"What? No!"

"No, you won't take care of me?"

The war on his face is obvious. "Luss. I can't ask that of you. Is that what he's demanding." He points in Lucifer's direction.

"I offered. I'll be like a human. Does that mean you won't take care of me? You'll put me in a home?"

"No, I... never. Not unless I'm right beside you. It's just, the thought of you dead, I can't..." He swallows and shakes his head.

I look at Lucifer. In my head, I ask, "That's the deal?"

He nods and shrugs.

Typical. I return my attention to Nick. "If I have to die, I'm okay with it. I'll find you wherever souls go after this world is finished. I don't want to live without you, Nick, not today and not in some unnamed number of years." I break our communion and look toward Lucifer again, the tears in my eyes blurring his outlines. "Can you give me a soul?" I ask out loud.

"No."

"Lucifer," Rose objects.

"You already have a soul, Lussi. All Kinds do, excepting ogres and some more ancient orcs, for obvious reasons. Vicious, immoral creatures. If it is your desire to find Nicholas after this life, I have little doubt that you will." He smiles, and this time, the twist of his lips holds kindness. "And I'll make it easier for you."

With a wave of his hand, Lucifer does something. I feel a siphoning off, although I can't explain it. It's like a stuttering that comes to a halt inside me. "There will be no children. No accidents. No intentional production. However, once you say your vows, Lussi, your life will be set to match Nicholas's. When he dies, so do you."

"Luss." Nick mourns and shakes his head. "No. That's unacceptable."

"Sshh." I lean in and brush a kiss over his lips. "It's what I want. And you already asked me to marry you, so unless you plan to be a liar, you'd better meet me on the altar and say those vows." I can tell he wants to object again, so to forestall that, I turn my attention back to The Devil. "And my magick?"

"Use it wisely, as we once agreed. Consider your retention of your gifts a wedding present from us. Now, if there's nothing else?"

"You'll tell Michael I'm allowed to stay above shell?"

"Done. Now, though I hate to rush along guests, I do have a crib to build. Insane, when I could just imagine it into existence, but..." He sighs before kissing his bride's forehead again.

He waves his hand... and we're back in Nick's bedroom.

"That went well." But when I turn to him, Nick is another shade of pale that doesn't exist in any human dictionary.

He flops to the floor, his legs giving out. Normally, I'd be embarrassed to be associated with such a wimp, but meeting Lucifer does tend to have a similar effect across all Kinds. I've seen vampires and gargoyles cavil on the floor after meeting the second most powerful being in all of Creation.

All that matters is I've won a life with Nick, and that's worth my immortality and an agreement never to have biological children.

I wonder how long my fiancé will remain on the floor. I'd like to celebrate...

CHAPTER NINETEEN:

Nick

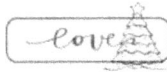

The week speeds by, even though time ticks with excruciating slowness as I try to avoid Lussi. Not avoid completely. Just in a physical sense.

Doing so without her noticing is impossible, so I'm lying through my teeth every other minute, with the ones spent in-between trying to come up with innovative excuses: my stomach hurts, I have a headache, patient meetings, still trying to catch up on work after my sojourn in Hell.

Not that any of it fools her, but I need to do something, anything, to stop my dick from doing more damage. Every single time I slip inside her, I fall more in love. I can't help but believe she must feel the same.

I've discovered there's a difference between fucking and having sex with someone you care about deeply. In the latter, the intimate act fuses two people together. *Making love.* I've heard it called that. I never realized the words for what they are: creating love. Binding love.

I've taken enough from my Winter Witch with my insane belief I could cure her. I kicked at the pediment upon which she stood. I'm so afraid I've made it too crumbly to hold her, just as she once accused next to the Sea of Elicher.

It seems like a lifetime ago.

"Nick? What are you doing?" Lussi walks into the bedroom, where I'm folding laundry on the bed.

Much to my own surprise, I've developed a neatness kick since I left Hell, though I don't always follow through. I still leave items lying around, but not nearly as many as I used to. But now, my newfound orderliness isn't due to personal growth. I can't say that having given so much therapy, I've received a bit of others' progressions on the backside.

No, the truth is, being neat now is a coping mechanism, a way to keep my Winter Witch close once I've broken us apart.

I can't breathe. Where did all the damned oxygen go in the room?

"Just trying to catch up on chores." Without meeting her eyes, I turn and place the folded tee-shirts into the dresser drawer before I return to matching and folding socks.

"You are?"

I can feel her wringing her hands in the doorway. Without looking, I know the way her forehead creases around her large third eye, but I can't turn around.

So when she slips up beside me and her hand reaches out to cover mine, I drop the socks and squinch my eyes shut.

"Nick? Please. Just talk to me. Aren't you the one who's always going on about communication?"

"You shouldn't listen to me. I don't know everything." Or anything, really.

"Do you know anything?"

I dart a glance her way to find her studying me, her lips pressed into a thin, impenetrable line. "No."

Slowly, she nods before she sinks to the bed. Taking up a pair of socks, she runs them through her fingers. "If you don't want to talk to me, then you can listen. This... avoidance... can't go on forever, Nick."

I take three pairs of socks from the pile and toss them in the dresser, anything to skirt the conversation I'm dreading. "Not many things can."

"Not us, anyway. We haven't even lasted two full months, have we?" The sorrow in her voice is so profound, tears spring to my eyes.

I swipe them away before I turn. "What are you trying to say?" But my heart is beating so loud, I can barely hear the words I'm saying.

She pats the spot next to her on the bed. "Sit. Please."

"I'd rather stand."

With a long sigh, she nods. "You might not know this about me. We talked a lot in Hell, but it takes longer than a few weeks to get to know everything about a person. Anyway, I haven't been completely sheltered. I've been in serious relationships, Nick. Not like now, not like what's between us, but I've felt strongly several times."

"You have?" Despite knowing that I'm going to leave her, a wave of green jealousy sweeps through me. "With whom?"

"Two warlocks, one demon. I never considered marrying any of them, but at the time, each relationship was important in its own way. I was fond of them, even thought at the time I might love them, until I wasn't and didn't." She shrugs. "I'm over fifteen hundred years old. I've been alone for so many centuries."

"But you said…"

"I said I've never loved as I love you, which is absolutely true. I've never felt this way about anyone else, not even close. I never realized that what I was feeling for them wasn't much more than a mix of attraction and liking. With you… with you, it's like breathing. Necessary. Sustaining. Impossible to put aside without serious consequences."

My shoulders ease and tense at the same time: ease, because I don't want her to have loved anyone else, even if it makes me a horrible person, and tense because her words rake like sharp daggers through my gut.

I'm such a jerk. I wish someone had told me so I could have warned her.

I clear my throat. "I've never been in love, either, Luss. Until you."

She nods, draws in a breath, and nods again. "If you had been, or I suppose, if you'd lived fifteen hundred years, you'd know that fifty years' after we've parted, you'll only be a bad memory to me. In a hundred years, you'll barely be a memory at all."

"Luss?" The daggers take swipes at my heart. My hand covers my chest, trying to push back the pain. What's she saying? How can she say these things?

"What happens," she continues, inexorable, unceasing, "is that the pain of parting overwhelms the happy times, especially when two people have loved for so short a period, like we have. You'll have to trust me on this one, since I'm immortal and you're not."

If my heart beats any faster, it will fly through my chest and drop to the floor like a ragged, bloody stump. "I don't understand." But I do.

"There's a course men follow when they wish to leave. Silence, less physicality, and attention to things like socks." She tosses a rolled-up ball into the air and whisks it into the drawer past me with her magick. Meeting my gaze, she asks, "Do you wish to leave me, Nick?"

No. Not a single part of me except for the tiny strand of a better man that's managed to shout and assert itself through the rest of my selfish desires. "It's..." My voice trails off. I can't do this.

I have to. For her. Because I love her. Because she deserves better from me than a death sentence. First, I tried to change her. Now, to love me she'll have to change one of the essential gifts of her creation.

Sinking next to her, I take her hand in mine and prepare to dissemble. "The thing is, I-I suddenly realized how serious we've become and how we don't really know that much about each other. I think, maybe, we've put the cart before the horse. If we could just take a step back, maybe date a bit, maybe see other people, I, um, I think it would be best." I flinch as I deliver the death knell of every relationship.

Silence beats too long, my ears filled only by the rapid-fire rhythm of my pulse and the unrelenting and unreleased sobs echoing inside my hollowed-out chest. An old alarm clock in the corner flips over the minute. I squeeze her hand... and let go.

Before I can rise, she speaks in a soft, modulated tone. "I know what you're doing.

Giving up immortality is my decision, Nick. And besides, it's not the loss you're thinking it is."

I round on her, taking her face between my palms. "You. Will. Die. You will grow old and become worm food. Don't tell me that's nothing. That's everything, Lussi. That's everything, and there's no way I deserve such a sacrifice, not when there's not an equal one I can give you in return."

And there it is, the truth vomited out, though I tried to keep it hidden.

"Which is why you won't touch me anymore."

"I'm touching you now."

She rips my hands from her face and throws them back at me. "Don't be an idiot. I deserve honesty, not some adolescent quip. Do you still want to fuck me, Nick?"

"Lussi!" I growl her name and run my hands through my hair. She's insistent on taking everything from my soul, but if she does, I'll have nothing left with which to fight for her life. She'll be able to argue me around to her point of view, since all I really want to do is to let her win.

"Do. You. Nicholas Frye. Want to fuck me? Lussi?" She enunciates the question, leaning in.

"Luss..."

"Do you? Answer me, Nick. Answer me like a man rather than whatever creature you're being right now. Answer like your heart depends upon it, as if your life hangs in the balance, the lives of every person on this benighted planet..."

"Yes!" I interrupt her, the response torn from me. "I want to fuck you. I want to wake up with you. I want to go to sleep cuddled around your soft skin and incredible heart. I want to live with you forever. I want to marry you and give you my last name, even if it's caveman of me to want it. I want you so much that I'm just about strong enough to let you go so you'll live, Lussi. So you'll continue to be who you are—The Winter Witch of Norway, a force of nature and et-ternal." My voice breaks on the last word. "I won't let you give up a single part of who you are."

"Won't let me?" she parrots. Shaking her head, she rises to her feet, looking so sad that tears begin to flow from my eyes again. "I never thought you were a coward, but I always knew you were enthralled by my magick. I guess keeping it isn't enough for you, not without the persona behind it."

"What do you mean?"

She shrugs. "It's like marrying a rock star, isn't it? There's some ancillary fame attached to the significant other, but that disappears when the musician ages out of popularity. When he or she can no longer sing the same notes."

"That's not…"

"You're a star-fucker, Nick, nothing more," she interrupts, her voice lined with contempt. "So maybe you're right. It's a good thing I found this out about you before we married. Supernatural divorces suck."

She disappears. One moment, she's there, the next, gone. I jump to my feet and rush through all the rooms, but she's disappeared. Not a trace of her remains except for the vague scent of storm and wildflowers—and her engagement ring on the kitchen counter.

I leave the ring where it is, a symbol of all I've lost.

***

After three days of walking around my apartment like a zombie, I make a startling realization: I'm an ass.

More than that, I've fallen into the same trap as countless others I've counseled. I've substituted my judgment for my partner's. And I've been hiding my own worst instincts beneath the desire to do good.

Because yes, I don't want Lussi to die, but she's right. Hidden within a small bend in my altruism is a not-insignificant upset that she won't be the force of nature she is right now. Part of the upset is that I don't want to change the least part of her. She's marvelous and perfect as she is. But the other part, the worst part, is that I like the idea of how I've tamed The Winter Witch of Norway. And can she be The Winter Witch if her lifespan is tied to mine?

I hate this part of me, but now that I examine it, I can see it for the fool's gold that it is. Now that I see it, I can love her without reservation.

Why have I been so worried about control? I don't have any. It doesn't matter. She's more powerful than me, more complex, and likely more capable. I don't have the right or the ability to dictate her decisions for her.

Lussi will always be exactly who she wants to be, and whoever that person is, human or witch, she's marvelous. If she loses limbs, develops an illness that leaves her vomiting and bedridden, or if she grows old and warty and smells like cat food, she's still going to be the woman I love.

But the realization changes nothing. I'm still alone. I sent her an email, but it bounced back. She must have closed her account. I set up an Instagram for her during the weeks below shell when I foolishly avoided taking her to bed, which I now regret with every pulse of my sad, drooping dick, but she's closed that account, too. I can fly back to Norway, but how would I transport down to Hell?

There's one way, but no one on earth would be dumb enough to try it. Then again, I'm feeling pretty stupid right now.

After showering for the first time in days, I grab my passport from the top drawer of my desk, send my secretary a message to cancel all appointments and reschedule those she can with the psychologist who usually covers for me, and call a ride.

The entire plane trip to Trinidad, I debate the wisdom of what I'm about to do, but I can't think of another way to get in touch with Lussi short of waiting nearly a year for her to ride with her horde above shell. That's my back-up plan: I can make a mess in a field and wait for her to show up to right it. Of course, she might kill me. Not only will she be annoyed at the disorder, she's got to be fuming at my idiocy in forcing her away.

When I land on the sweltering airstrip, I chug across the tarmac towards the building where I hope to catch one of the puddle-hopper planes to Tobago. Heat swirls around me, hotter than anything I encountered with Lussi in Hell.

My grip on my carry-on bag, the only thing I've brought with me, slips. I scramble to catch it with sweaty palms, and as I do, I stagger—right into a rock wall. My head bounces off, and a hand grips my arm before I can splay on the tarmac and receive first-degree burns.

"Nicholas Frye. I appreciate the effort at coming to visit, but I don't wish Rose to become upset by your idiocy. She'll feel sorry for Lussi, which will unsettle her, and being unsettled isn't good for either my bride or my baby. Or my temper." Lucifer smiles. There isn't any wickedness or malevolence in the expression. There's only a man looking out for his wife's sensibilities.

"How did you...?"

"Know? *Tch.*" He clicks his tongue against his teeth. "You're right. You're an ass, and you don't deserve her. On the other hand, who am I to stand in the way of true love?" He cocks his head. "You'll find her where you picnicked first. Don't mess this up."

With a flicker of his fingers, the world disappears and another takes its place. I find myself in Lussi's bedroom below shell. After staggering from the travel, I drop my bag.

Place where we picnicked. Got it. I don't bother to look around the room. Instead, I rush outside and race down the path through the woods, dodging the various trees and foliage until I hear the distant sound of water splashing and stop to get my bearings. I think we went right... or left. Or straight. At the time, I was so overwhelmed by Lussi that I didn't take note of geography.

Turning in a circle, I squint down five paths. Two look as if they haven't been used in a while, but with time running differently below shell, I'm not sure if that matters. I wrack my brain, trying to remember which direction we traveled. Finally, I eenie-meenie-miney-moe it, which leads me to the left.

I don't normally worry about choices, but right now, I'm hyperventilating. I speed down the left path until I dead-end in rows of brambles. Irritated with the lost time, I retrace my steps and decide to follow the middle path. As I round the first curve, I hear a shuffling, grunting sound. My heart and feet stutter to a stop.

The leaves rustle just ahead. A high-pitched whine pierces the air. A low rumble follows, and the foliage parts around a giant cat the size of a horse. It's sleek and black, shiny, with golden eyes narrowed upon me. Head swinging back and forth, gaze trained, it pads its way closer to me. I see death in the long saber-like teeth dripping saliva like acid tears.

I don't even have my backpack. I have nothing with which to protect myself. Maybe this was Lucifer's plan all along. He wanted me out of Lussi's life. Permanently.

"G-good cat. N-nice cat," I stutter, backing up slowly, my hand extended towards it.

But it continues pacing towards me, ears held flat against its head. My foot trips on some roots, and I stumble. When I right myself, the cat is there, so close, I feel its breath on my fingers. It opens its mouth and snarls, fetid death waiting.

My life flashes before me as I lower my hand and close my eyes. At least Lussi will live forever.

But instead of fangs closing around my throat, I feel a long, sandpapery tongue lick up my neck and past my cheekbone. When I peek open one eye, I see the cat about to butt its head into my stomach. When it does, I trip backward and land on my ass. The cat quickly covers me, all four legs surrounding my torso as it snuffles at the crook in my neck.

Laughter, bright and sunny, rings out over the path. "You so deserve that, Nicholas Frye. Jorgi, move. You're going to give Nick a heart attack." Lussi's hand extends past the cat to help me to my feet. I grab it, never so happy to see her as I am right now, for so many reasons.

"You've gotten a pet?" I don't bother brushing myself off. All I can see is her.

"No. Jorgi's just visiting from Iceland. She's the daughter of my friend. Jorgi, meet Nick. Nick, Jorgi."

The cat raises its paw. Left with little other to do, I shake it, but I keep my eyes on Lussi the whole time.

"You're so beautiful. Your hair."

She raises the hand not holding mine and strokes it over her shorter cut. Instead of long tresses, she now sports a bob that brushes her shoulders in an even line. With her delicate bones, she looks more fragile and feminine than ever. "Do you like it?"

"I do. But then, I like everything about you."

She rolls her eyes. "Is that your apology? If so, I'm tempted to leave you to Jorgi's tender attentions."

The cat has sunk to her haunches and started a bath, but at her name, she looks up. She doesn't have eyebrows, but I swear she raises them in question.

"Never mind, Jorgi. Don't let me interrupt your ablutions." I pull Lussi into my arms. When her fingers begin tracing my pecs, a thrill of relief rushes through me. "I'm going to tell Lussi how much I adore her, what a total ass I've been, and how I will worship her from here to whenever she dies with me. And that, if she never does magick again, it's okay. If she doesn't want to marry me, it's okay. We'll live together, or we'll date. I hope we'll do and be something to each other, because all I want is to wake up to her smile each morning and go to sleep with her wrapped against me each night, however long it takes me to convince her to forgive me."

A smile the size of Texas breaks over Lussi's face. "As apologies go, that's not terrible. Now say it to me."

"The essentials are that I've been an ass, and I'll do anything to be with you. And yes, I know I'm promising a supernatural entity carte blanche, and I don't care. Because I trust you. I love you."

She taps my chest. "Still not a good idea, but yes, you're safe with me. I'd destroy myself before harming you, Nick. You must know that."

"I think I do, because that's how I feel about you." I pause and stroke my thumbs over her cheekbones. "I still can't think of you dying without wanting to slit my wrists, but I suppose if your life is tied to mine, and if you're truly okay with that, then I'll be dying with you. And maybe that's the best outcome any two people in love can hope for."

"About time you realized it."

I press my lips against hers, and when she melts and opens to me, I'm filled with a sense of peace. This. This is what coming home is all about.

As our kiss deepens, I run my hands down her curves before I grab the back of her neck, holding her to me. Her nipples pebble under my touch as a groan slips from my lips through hers.

But in a quick movement, she uses her magick to back me against a tree. Hands made of wind rip my clothing from my body. My shirt shreds. My belt unwinds. My trousers rip along the seams. Even my socks, shoes, and underwear disappear into the ethers.

And my dick, free, presses against her and finds heat and soft skin.

I'm just angling my knees when a loud, grating, tearing clap of a noise stalls us both.

"Fuck!" In one move, instinct kicking in, I rotate Lussi back against the tree and I slide in front of her. A cloud of light and lightning supercharges the forest before it begins resolving into the form of an ancient warrior.

An enormous warrior, so fierce and mighty, the ground shakes around him. He wears metal armor etched with winged lions and covered in gold. Some sort of masculine skirt swirls around his bare, muscled legs. His feet are encased in gilded sandals. A flow of red fabric chases down the being's back, much like a Roman soldier's cape, but this man carries no weapons or shield. Above bulging biceps that make mine look like ant hills, swarthy skin gives way to long hair tipped with gold.

He's... awesome. Power expels from him in waves that hold me frozen.

"Get down, Nick," Lussi hisses. Beside me rather than behind as she should be, she sinks to her knees, arms stretched in front of her, the top of her head pressed to the ground.

What the hell?

A wave of her magick hits me in my knees as she hisses again. I fall to the earth, but I can't stop looking at the figure in front of me. Enormous power, yes, but a gentle expression.

"Your Majesty." Tremors run up and down Lussi's limbs. The vibration of her movement shakes my knees.

The being winks at me, a small smile playing over his lips. "Rise, Winter Witch. And—here." He waves his hand, and I'm suddenly clothed in a white robe. "I know how you humans value modesty."

Lussi, who scrambles to her feet, has been similarly garbed. She reaches for my elbow to help me stand, not that I need help. I'm not the one terrified at the moment.

"I suppose my timing might have been better," he murmurs, but there's a twinkle in his bright blue eyes. They're similar to Lucifer's in their glowing light and pure color.

Archangel Michael. I'm sure of it. There's only a vague family resemblance to

Lucifer except for the similar eyes and majesty, but the same sense of impossible energy makes my skin tingle.

I pull Lussi into my side as I nod at the celestial entity. She's shaking, terrified, my witch who didn't bother giving The Devil the slightest obeisance. But she's wary of the archangel.

But I'm not. He's an angel. What's the worst he can do?

"Quite a bit, actually, Nicholas Frye." He responds to my thought, loosing a larger trickle of power. It sweeps over the earth around us like a ground storm and bends the thickest trees low before he snaps it back. "But happily for you, I hold humans close to my heart."

I nod. Myth calls him the protector of humanity, but I've learned in recent days that myth is mostly wrong. Still, I sense a kindness and compassion in him that I didn't in Lucifer.

"My brother sent a message indicating you'll want a ceremony performed," he continues, looking at Lussi. "Heaven help me if I don't jump at my youngest sibling's command." His lips twist with the sarcasm.

I hold Lussi tighter to my side as I process the words. "You're going to marry us?"

"No one closer to Heaven than me, human. Winter Witch? What say you? And think carefully before you respond. Once the vows are said, there is no going back, and you will no longer be welcome below shell."

Carefully, I rotate Lussi's face towards mine, and wait until her three eyes leave Michael to meet my own. But her gaze keeps slipping, trying to keep Michael in her sights as if he's a wild beast capable of attacking.

"Luss? Eyes here." I tap the space between mine to focus her attention. She smiles at the reminder of our first meeting, but her gaze stays on me. "Will you marry me, Luss, even though I'm a fool and messy and completely unworthy of you and your sacrifice?"

"Got that right," she snorts, but her eyes soften. She runs her trembling finger over my lips, tracing their outline. "Yes, Nick. I'll marry you. I don't want to just live with you. I want it all: the vows, the ring, and the lifetime together, with death that comes at its end."

"Wonderful!" Michael claps his hands, the sound like thunder, interrupting our tender scene just as I'm about to lean down and kiss Lussi once more. "Now, let's get this party on the road."

With a wave of his hand, twinkling lights appear strung between branches, a riot of flowers bloom in a half-circle around us, and green-leafed wreaths of some kind are plopped on our heads.

"Lussi, do you, The Winter Witch of Norway, take this miserable excuse of a human—you know I'm right, Nicholas Frye, and I'm expecting better of you from now on—to be your wedded mate, whatever comes, until the end of your days?"

Lussi tips her chin to meet my gaze. "I do," she whispers softly.

"Wonderful. And you, Nicholas Frye, do you promise Lussi your hearth, your nurture, your heart, and your home, until your days end?"

"I do."

"Then, by the power vested in me, by me, I pronounce you husband and wife. You may now get on with the kissing and the expression of true love I so unfortunately interrupted." But a wide smile crosses his features. "Congratulations upon your union." He pauses and sobers. "Three days, Lussi, and you must vacate your abode below shell. I cannot have mortals traipsing all over the realm. It isn't safe."

But before Lussi can agree, I cover her mouth with mine. This kiss is different from any other we've shared. This kiss has forever stamped across its width. This kiss marks her as mine, and me as hers.

Jorgi meows and proceeds to give herself a bath.

CHAPTER TWENTY:

December 12-13 – *Lussi*

Our apartment looks amazing and smells even better. It's like Nick on steroids, but with the added enticement of sugar cookies, fir, and hot cocoa. Fronds of fresh greenery line the fireplace mantle and grace the door. We've decorated a tree with his grandmother's glass ornaments and little twinkling lights we bought together at the store. Candles provide flickering flames around the room. It's been dark for hours in Norway, but here, in Connecticut, the gray light still seeps through the windows.

It's not just between realms that Time runs afoul of itself.

Outside, snow falls. Inside, Christmas carols play. I particularly like the current one. The tune is upbeat, and the lyrics relate the details of an accident between a grandmother and a reindeer. I'm sure the grandmother deserved it. Probably crossed the street without looking both ways first.

I snicker at my thoughts. I'm still The Winter Witch. I still appreciate rules and order. I've changed, but maybe not as much as Nick hopes. On this, my day, my violent streak is showing. The other days of the year it hides, but today it makes itself known in little ways.

I need to ride. It's who I am.

Nick hands me a red and white candy cane. We're placing them on the tree at staggered intervals, enjoying the last five minutes before my demon horde arrives to fetch me. Nick keeps glancing at the clock on the wall, his frown growing with every passing minute.

"I'll know the time. It's in my blood."

He nods and doesn't respond. He's trying to keep our night festive. It's our first real Christmas season together since we didn't celebrate last year while I kept him as my prisoner—houseguest—in Hell. It's unfortunate that the fear I mean to slaughter and kill makes my new husband anxious. He's ruining our merry, jolly moments together.

I blow out a long breath, tamping down again on the corkscrew of antipathy brewing inside me. My night calls, like nails scratching across a chalkboard.

With five minutes left until my personal witching hour, demons pop up all around us. Even knowing they'd arrive, Nick startles and drops the box of canes he's holding.

Sami bends to pick them up before bowing to me. He hands them to Nick. "Sir. Apologies. Didn't mean to frighten you. Lady, are we ready to ride?"

"We are." I place my last cane with care.

"Luss. Please." Nick catches me by the waist and turns me into him. Even after so many days and nights in his bed, I melt. I thought the lust I felt for him would fade. If anything, it's doubled.

"Trust me, Nicholas Frye." I stroke his stubbled jaw before dragging his lips to mine in a hot, wet kiss. I let my mouth make the silent promise before I break away.

To my delight, his hands clasp tighter around me, and his dick strains against his pants.

"Sami," I say over my shoulder, "we ride. But I need to be home in time for the movie, so we're not staying out all night."

Nick wants to show me a bunch of animated films from the sixties. He says I'm going to love them. One of them is about Rudolph, who's already become my favorite hero. He looks strange, like me, and he wins love and respect in the end. Nick and I are planning to warm ourselves by the fire in the grate while we stare at the tree, eat popcorn, drink cocoa, and try not to cry. That's what Nick says, anyway.

I return my attention to my husband. "Make sure to stir the *fårikål* every quarter hour. The flame is low, but it will still burn if you're not careful. And the timer is set for the *eplekake.*" But baking requires precision, and I'm not sure I can trust Nick. "When you hear the buzzing, you have to remove the pan and set it on the stand right away. No dawdling."

"I won't burn the cake," he promises.

"Or the meal."

"Or the meal," he repeats. "Do you really have to go?"

"It's my job."

"Your job is to organize people's lives."

He's not wrong. I've opened my own business, *Witch Without A Broomstick,* which provides organizational consultant services. So far, I've helped three women and five men put order to their clutter and lives. None of them know who I am. I've cut my hair, so my bangs lay heavy across my forehead, hiding my eye. In private, I use a barrette to hold back my hair, but when I mix in public, I prefer to pretend that I'm human. It just makes life easier. Plus, I've lived fifteen hundred years on the outskirts of every society. I want to fit in, for once.

But my avocation still requires that I ride with my horde. We're going to do things a little bit differently this year, though. "I'll tell you all about my night when I return."

He kisses me again, hungry and yearning. I taste his trepidation as well as the way he swallows it.

To his credit, he's become a nearly perfect husband. When I need advice, like when I started my business and had to learn all about human laws and regulations, he helped enormously. But when I wish to do things on my own, he bites his lip, nods, and let's me go. I know it's not easy for a bossy pants like him, but he's managing.

Plus, unlike most men, he likes to hear about all my inner thoughts. Marrying a therapist was a good move from the conversational perspective. He prefers talking to almost any other activity.

Almost.

"Be safe, Mrs. Frye."

My newish last name still sends thrills through me.

When Nick backs slowly away, I gather the cords of my demons and drag them through the ethers back to Norway. We land on the banks of the fjord. I magick burlap sacks and long sticks and hand them around.

"This is our new routine. We're going to cross the country and pick up litter, thereby cleaning and organizing our land, but in a modern way. When your sacks are full, bring them back to me, here." I magick them each a piece of paper with the address of the recycling center printed on it. "I'm trusting you not to sow chaos. If any disappoint me, he will not be allowed out next year. The demon with the most litter collected will win a special prize."

That stalls their querulous whining. Demons are nothing if not competitive. Still, it takes another twenty minutes before they disperse. Once they do, I take a deep breath and pop over to the orphanage where six children remain in care.

By the time my demons return with their first sacks, I've deposited the little ones back to their homes. There's two I still worry over. The houses where they will live still show signs of dissipation and neglect. I've lectured those parents. Terrorized them, really. I'll have to check on the children during the year to make certain they're being well cared for.

A sigh escapes me as a long breath of air as I slip back to the recycling center. I made mistakes. I can see that now. Though the children I took were never harmed, though they lived easy, happy, joyful lives in the orphanage, and though many have since grown into strong, capable, and caring adults, taking them from their families wasn't right.

What's a Winter Witch to do with her own past crimes and the disorder and pain she's strewn into the world? I don't know. I can't turn back time. I tried, without success, once I saw Nick's reaction to my admission and suddenly realized the agony I'd been causing. I'm hoping therapy will help me find a way to right my wrongs.

Guilt is a difficult emotion for me. Those clawing cats in my chest are...

unpleasant. But as I've learned from Mrs. Olstad, guilt is a goad to do better. She tells me that embracing the emotion will help me find a way to balance the destruction I've caused. And since guilt is a human emotion that monsters never feel, I'm beginning to welcome the clawing, drowning, itching sensations because I don't want to be a monster anymore. At least, not on the inside. Not where it counts.

Six hours later, my demons and I meet. Together, we sort and clean the recyclables before making a pit stop at the garbage dump for the waste that's impossible to re-use.

A feeling of utter contentment fills me as the last sled of refuse is deposited into the giant hole in the ground. Cleaning the beautiful earth of litter isn't what I expected I'd wish to do with my night, but I've always loved the world above shell. The colors, the smells, the sights. Righting what humans have wronged with their carelessness is my new obsession.

When I zap us back to Connecticut, Nick jumps off the couch. The book he's been reading, or pretending to read, if I know him—and I do—tumbles to the floor. He rushes to me and sweeps me up in his strong arms.

"I missed you so much." He plants kisses along my cheeks, my lips, and my forehead around where my eye rests. "I was so worried. And your skin is chill like winter air."

"Because we've been out of doors. But see? We're safe and unharmed." I'll tell him about our night later. Right now, I want dinner and my promised movies.

Sami steps forward. "Who won, Lady? And what's the prize?"

"The prize is Christmas dinner with Nick, his mother, his cousins and aunts and uncles, and me. And the winner is... all of you."

I'm not sure how Mama Frye and family will handle dinner with my horde, but judging by the way they jump and congratulate each other, my demons are excited. Only Razmig looks crestfallen. He outdid himself with twenty-six sleds.

"And for Razmig, who collected the most trash," I add, capturing their attention, "he's going to have the privilege of opening a present from under the tree on Christmas morning."

The chaos that follows as the horde begins to take out their jealousy on the winner is something I don't want to deal with, so I wave them all back to Hell. If they kill each other, there will be more Christmas pudding for the rest of us.

Nick is making sounds I've never heard, and when I return my attention to him, he's sputtering, gurgling, and laughing, all at the same time. "I'd better call Mom. Can your magick disguise how they look?"

"I can glamour them, sure, at least for a couple hours." Long enough, anyway, to keep the Frye family sane, although I'm not quite certain how to police their manners.

That's tomorrow's problem.

"And build a table long enough to feed them all?"

I love him even when he's unattractive, like now, and questioning my abilities.

But I love him even more when, later, after we've finished the movies that made me cry and the *fårikål* and *eplekake* have been decimated, he leads me to the bedroom.

He's more demanding than usual. When I try to tease him and pull back, he locks his lips on mine and proceeds to suck me into him once more. His fingers pluck at my nipples, already hard as stone.

There's something about this man. Others have touched me in all the right places. He touches my soul.

I bend to his caresses and melt beneath my skin. With a sharp move, he rips his lips from mine. The pretty gray dress I'm wearing follows. The tear echoes through the room.

If I wore panties, they'd be soaked.

I start to sink to my knees, wanting to taste him, but he stops me. Instead, he pushes me onto the bed and covers me.

"Get rid of the clothes."

It's an order, and when I comply, he hums. It's a silent accolade, and I swear, I almost come.

He presses kisses over my bare chest, sucking in my nipple, and pushes me to the peak barreling down upon me like an avalanche. I can't escape it or soften the hard, acid edges of the storm, especially when he reaches between my legs and finds my clit. Pinching it, he sends me hurtling over the edge with a long cry.

I sound like a banshee. When I tremble back to earth, I blink up at Nick, whose hazel eyes burn with a swirl of color.

"Good girl."

And I cum again. It's a rush of slick between my legs as he praises me. I'm a dangerous, monstrous creature. He makes me liquefy with mere words.

His hard length slides through my folds, and with only the briefest pause, Nick slips inside me. The stretch never falters. I gasp as my walls pulse through the orgasm I haven't yet come down from. With a growl, he wiggles even deeper, maybe the deepest he's ever gone, as if his dick has grown three inches.

Pain? Pleasure? My body devolves into shuddering ripples that rush through my blood.

"Fuck, you're perfect," he whispers before tipping back his head and inhaling through his nose. When he looks at me again, there's fire in his eyes. "Here?" he asks, moving slowly over the quivering spot. "Or, here?" He moves a millimeter up, and I mewl with the sensation. "There," he agrees with a devilish smile.

Tilting back his hips, he rolls into me, taking care to brush over the spot. As I suck in air in huge gasps, he hisses and squints shut his eyes.

"More," I plead.

He drags back his hips and rolls them into my upthrust. Once, twice, and then the savage strain upon his features twists as he hisses my name. His seed spurts hot and profound inside me, leading me to another orgasm that tightens me around him until he growl-cries and pulses again.

After, we rest side by side, sweat cooling on our skins, hearts returning back to a more normal beat. He laughs. "I can't believe how lucky I am."

"I'm the lucky one." I turn over on my side. "Have you decided what to do about your presentation?"

This coming February, he's giving the keynote speech in Switzerland to his inquisitive fellow mental helpers. He's back and forth on the supernatural aspect and what he should reveal or not reveal. I've asked him not to use me or what he's learned through me for two reasons. First, no one will believe him unless he opens me up for scientific testing, which neither of us wants. Second, the supernatural isn't supposed to be revealed to the world. He agrees.

"I'm going to do what I should have done last year when you swept into my room on a whirlwind and changed my life. I'm going to discuss the uptick in reports of monsters across the globe and offer DSM-5 possible explanations. I'll leave it to each of my audience to determine whether the facts match the criteria."

"Which they don't."

He rolls to his side as well and brushes my hair off my face. "Can't cure stupidity or blindness, I suppose, but some in the audience will begin to see that the emerging patterns don't match our simplistic understanding of how the world works."

"And that's enough for you?"

"You're enough for me, Luss. Everything else is just... window dressing." He chuckles suddenly. "Besides, I was wrong about trying to wrap you up in a DSM-5 category. You're more than a disorder." He pauses. "Maybe everyone is. We're told to use a patient's background to inform our diagnoses, but we rarely do. It's too easy to believe our little charts are gods before which everyone and everything must bow."

I nod. "I did the same thing. I thought the world had to bow to my interpretation of how it should be run. And look what happened."

"You can't change who you were, Luss. You can only change who you'll be. The same holds for me, by the way."

I nod again. Easier said than done, but in the platitude is a kernel of truth. Going forward, it's up to me to decide whether I'll be a monster or not. How I was born and how I look doesn't have to mean my life and choices will forever be imprisoned by those parameters.

Nick's fingers trill along my skin. "I've been thinking about a slightly different approach to therapy."

"Oh?"

"I'm not going to try to 'cure' anyone. I'm going to teach people to recognize motivations, that will be the same, but instead of attempting to change personalities to fit in with society's expectations, we're going to find workarounds."

"Like my forcing my horde to clean the earth rather than knocking down chimneys. I'm still Lussi of the Long Night, The Winter Witch. My need to right the world is just expressed in a different, more productive manner."

He pauses. "Is that what you did? Picked up trash?"

"I'll tell you about it later. Finish explaining about the new therapy." Because I can't help thinking, he's making drastic changes to his profession because of me. That's like the ultimate "good girl" in action form.

"A lot of therapy is about becoming 'sane.' The problem is, I'm no longer certain what sanity means. I'm not sure any of us do, especially given the nature of the world is so different to what we're taught to believe."

"Got that right."

He spreads more kisses over my cheeks before subsiding and resuming his thoughts. "I think it's enough to teach my patients the rules and how to follow the rules, understand why the rules are important for society, and for the rest, just try to keep growing as complex individuals in a complex world."

"I have complete faith in you," I tell him, because it's true. He had faith in me, and as a result, my entire life cracked open and allowed in promise, hope, and love. Sure, I still straighten edges, but I no longer worry about perfection. For instance, I'm not picking up Nick's aftershave that he left by his computer.

I'll do it later.

Because I have an impossible perfection with Nick. Imperfect perfection is so much nicer than what I was trying to achieve.

Jorgi, our new black kitten, named after my friend's child who took a liking to Nick in Hell, jumps on the bed. With some pawing and scratching, she makes a nest in the small space between our necks and begins purring.

"Must you get between us, cat?" Nick snaps the question and pretends to be annoyed, but he ruins the simulation when he pats the kitten's head with soft fingers.

"I must." Jorgi purrs in cat-accented English.

To Nick's credit, he doesn't jump off the bed. Instead, he sighs, levers his head over the cat's long body that spills out from the indent between us, and kisses my lips before lying back and closing his eyes. In several moments, his breathing turns deep and even.

I watch over him until Jorgi tells me she'll remain vigilant. Only then do I close my eyes too and drift off into sleep, content to let my new familiar keep watch.

What? I'm still The Winter Witch of Norway. Now that I've finally found perfection, I intend to guard it with everything in me.

THE END

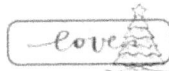

AN INTERESTING BUT NOT-VERY-SCHOLARLY DISCOURSE ON LUSSI

Or, some random thoughts I'm sharing because Lussi is fascinating and I wanted to understand why she's considered evil

Ah, Lussi! Where to begin, except with my belief that like so many strong, independent, outspoken, and frustrated women throughout history, she's been maligned and felled by male scribes and storytellers. She's been consigned only one night on which to ride and constrained by patriarchal societies to mute her power.

Is she truly a monster, or only made to bear a monster's guise?

Let's begin with the generally accepted version of who Lussi is: a witch, possibly a demon, possibly a vette/vaettir (a female spirit), but definitely a supernatural entity you won't wish to meet as the night of December 12th turns over into December 13th, the old Winter Solstice. On this night, Lussi Langnatt, Lussi Long Night, Lussi rides with her horde, (the Lussiferda, traditionally consisting of all sorts of mythological creatures), across Norway, and causes incalculable damage to anyone caught out of bed, outside, or whose chores have not been completed. That's her in a nutshell, but there's so much more.

Many Yule (Jul) traditions in Scandinavia have been handed down from pre-Christian times, and Lussi Langnatt is one of the most terrifying. The time spanning Lussi Langnatt and Yule Day (Juleaften-- Christmas) allows evil beings (evil spirits, trolls, the dead, etc.) an entry into our world so they might walk the frozen earth. To be outside during this period is dangerous, but on Lussi Langnatt the peril is greatest. In fact, tradition insists that someone in each household remain awake all night to guard the house against her. Over time, this tradition (Lussevaka) became a great excuse to hold all-night parties.

And no, don't look too closely at why parties would keep Lussi and her horde away, but she'll knock down your chimney if you're out of bed. Maybe all the parties take place in bed?

That's a different monster romance...

Hanging knives, axes, or scissors over doorways will also keep Lussi away. Post-Christianity, painting crosses is said to repel her entry.

Lussi doesn't like naughty children. She's liable to fly down the chimney and abduct them. Before going to bed on the eve of December 13th, children write Lussi's name on doors, walls, and fences in the hopes of appeasing her... vanity? Perhaps it's a dare, like whistling past graveyards.

Lussi also becomes enraged with those who leave tasks incomplete, especially chores necessary to create a festive Yule celebration. Work, such as threshing, slaughtering, cleaning, and spinning yarn must be completed to a high standard before her night and the commencement of the holiday season. Similarly, since animals are given the power of speech on this night, you'd best be good to them, or they'll call down Lussi on you. Lussi will smash down your chimney.

And should you be fool enough to venture outside on Lussi Langnatt, you might almost certainly encounter one of Lussi's minions who will just as easily kidnap you as look at you. Sometimes, those taken are simply transported elsewhere and left to find their way back home. Others disappear forever.

Lussi's ride with her horde has been theorized to be a version of the Wild Hunt (the Scandinavian Oskoreia) found across North, West, and Central Europe (and since this is its own topic upon which I could write an entire novel, I'll leave you only with the general idea that a ghostly leader and his hunters (the dead, some elves, or fairies) troll the skies, hunting). However, where the Oskoreia's leader is feared, he's not maligned like Lussi is. Think: he's so confident/she's such a bitch. An important point—to Lussi.

Now... some questions. No need to shout. I hear you asking, and I'm here to try to give you a succinct-ish version of what I think I've discovered.

First, you ask, why do I write that the Winter Solstice is December 13th when all people, everywhere, know the Solstice is December 21st? The answer is... because. Snafus aplenty occurred with the changing of the Julien to Gregorian calendar in or about 1700. Time itself was screwed up in magnificent fashion. There's still some discussion as to the actual Solstice date in the Julien calendar (December 12-14, pick your date, any date). However, most accept that the Winter Solstice occurred on December 13th, so as a result, Lussi rides the night as the 12th revolves into the 13th.

But is that true?

My first gut reaction was to question why Lussi's night wasn't similarly moved to December 21st with the changing of the calendar systems. After all, she's supposed to ride on the Solstice. But then I got to thinking about the number 13, and how interesting it is that a horrifying female is associated with the most horrifying number.

Let's talk about 13.

Triskaidekaphobia is defined as a fear of the number 13, and this fear has historical/mythological underpinnings in Norway (and elsewhere, of course).

In the Christian background, people point to the Last Supper and Judas the Betrayer's late arrival, marking 13 persons at this fateful final meal, as the reason 13 resonates so poorly with us. Plus, let's not forget those poor Templar knights who were rounded up (to be later burned) on October 13th.

The Biblical scholar, Godwin-Goziem-Jireh, states that although the Bible never says outright that 13 is an unlucky or evil number, he lists many examples of the number corresponding to rebellion within the pages.

Pre-Christian civilization, however, also deemed 13 unlucky. There was the time when Loki, the trickster god of Norway, crashed a party in Valhalla. With his arrival, 13 gods were gathered in one place. Of course, misery followed. Loki tricked Hodr, who was blind, into shooting a mistletoe-poisoned arrow into his brother, Balder. Balder, the god of joy, light, and goodness, was killed. From that moment to this, a gathering of 13 is considered unlucky. So is the number.

The number is also associated with female power, and while once 13 was sacred, it's devolution at the hands of a male-dominated cultural shift is one more reason it's considered an evil number.

In pre-Christian goddess-worshipping cultures, the number 13 wasn't unlucky. It was... everything... because it was associated with fertility. It was a link to the lunar and menstrual cycles per year (generally, these events are said to occur 13 times per year). In ancient times, fertility was highly prized. Art was created to celebrate the fecund female.

Take the Venus of Laussel. The 25,000-year-old limestone carving depicts a female (possibly a fertility goddess) with pendulous breasts and pregnant belly. While cradling her stomach with one hand, she holds aloft a horn with thirteen crescent-shaped cuts in the other. Most scholars believe the 13 cuts symbolize her menstrual cycle and feminine power.

But that was when women, scholars postulate, controlled their society. Things changed.

In ancient Greece, most definitely a male-controlled, patriarchal society, menstrual cycles were considered powerful, sure, but not in a good way. Pliny the Elder in his Natural History, published in 77 B.C.E., said of menstrual blood, "Contact with it turns new wine sour, crops touched by it become barren, [...] hives of bees die." (Ava Colleran, see https://pdxscholar.library.pdx.edu... cited below).

So, while Pliny the Elder also opined that a menstruating female walking naked could scare away windstorms, hail, and lightning, or even pests from corn, should she be traipsing unclothed through fields, her power hailed from darkness. It was bad.

And if female power is bad, if 13 is bad, and if Lussi's temperament and actions are bad... why not combine them? Why not combine them all into one night, so as to control and restrain everything associated with female power?

Perhaps I'm way off, but it seems to me that Lussi's awesome and fearful female power, like menstruation, like the number 13, is a threat to patriarchal civilization. I'm left wondering if part of her maligned notoriety and the continuation of her ride on the 13th rather than the 21st is because her extraordinary and fearful spiritual power needs to be contained. She's only allowed to ride one night a year: the 13th, where unlucky things go to dwell.

But she's also contained and constrained by her antithesis, St. Lucia, whose day she shares. More, below.

First, I want to talk about something else I noticed. Lussi's name means "Light."

What? Just like Lucifer?

Yes, exactly. And my research into him for Marked and Transcended also revealed an entity similarly maligned. Do I know what the similarity means? No. Am I interested? Yes. Maybe you will be, too.

First, I should remind that the Bible speaks of the number 13 in association with rebellion, not evilness, though in Lucifer's case, his rebellion devolved into an association with evil. And, though Lucifer is not directly mentioned in connection with the number 13 anywhere in the Bible, he is most definitely rebellion personified. But isn't Lussi as well? She demands order, but in performing her flight of rage, she rebels against the order maintained throughout the rest of the year. She's a rebellion against the norm.

Originally, Lucifer was portrayed as an adversary, someone to throw stones and obstacles in the road, but not an entity inherently evil. At least, not traditionally (what his myths became is a subject of a different conversation). Like Lussi, Lucifer is associated with the Darkness, yet his name and his beginnings show him to be a being of Light, an archangel. He's the duality carved in one body, but he also stands in opposition to what is Good and Light.

Like Lucifer, Lussi is made to stand as the opposition of Good and Light. Like him, she is named for Light even though she is associated with Darkness.

There, the similarity ends, and Lussi is given the ultimate disrespect. Where myth paints Lucifer's opposite as the Archangel Michael, more recent Christian myth paints Lussi's opposite as St. Lucia. And St. Lucia's Day is celebrated in Norway on... you guessed it... December 13th. And, where Lucifer's myth originally described him in a not-so-terrible light, Lussi's has, to the best of my knowledge, always written her as dangerous and evil, someone to be shunned and avoided. In fact, she's given such short shrift, she's even made to share her day with her antithesis, St. Lucia.

On December 13th, female power has been divided into two extremes (Lussi and Lucia), and therefore contained. Neutralized by Duality. Is it any wonder that Lussi is annoyed when she's been associated with bad luck (13), and made to split the only time that is rightfully hers with her nemesis?

Though, to be fair, St. Lucia is celebrated during the day of December 13th. Lussi is "celebrated" during the night leading to that day. Perhaps we might say that St. Lucia's light overcomes Lussi's darkness, a herald of hope for mankind when the freeze of winter begins to give way to longer days and warmer weather. The Solstice.

Still, not a boon to Lussi, who once again plays the part of the maligned whore to St. Lucia's reinterpretation of the Madonna. Once again, Lussi is restrained and constrained by the virgin/whore dichotomy. Her ability to own her power is restrained and constrained by St. Lucia cutting off her time abroad.

To be honest, I feel sorry for Lussi. What force might she wield in a matriarchal world, a world where duality is unnecessary? Yes, Lussi brings chaos with her, and nobody sane likes chaos, but that's often where evolution sprouts and grows.

Anyway, that's Lussi in a nutshell. Forgive the ramblings. I'm attaching some of my sources, below. As this isn't an academic paper, you'll have to bear with the absence of footnotes and some less-than-stellar sources (and yes, some rambling). I found these websites very interesting. You might, too.

Happy Reading Monster Lovers!

https://mythology.net/norse/norse-concepts/the-wild-hunt/

https://www.norwegianamerican.com/on-the-darkest-day-a-tale-of-two-lucys/

https://www.cnn.com/style/article/why-friday-13-unlucky-explained/index.html

https://www.ingvildeiring.com/project/lussi-langnatt-the-most-dangerous-night-of-the-year/

https://bladehoner.wordpress.com/2017/12/11/lussi-long-night/

https://greencanticle.com/tag/lussi-cats/

https://www.name-doctor.com/meaning/lussi

https://en.wikipedia.org/wiki/Culture_and_menstruation

https://www.quora.com/profile/Godwin-Goziem-Jireh

https://pdxscholar.library.pdx.edu/cgi/viewcontent.cgi?article=1263&context=younghistorians

ABOUT THE AUTHOR

Roslyn St. Clair lives a life of uninspired normalcy waiting for true magick to happen, which is why she has always chosen a second life in imagination.

Though she writes historical and modern romance another name, the author finds her first love in Dark Paranormal Romance and Monster Romance. Spending her days researching archangels, the devil, demons, angels, leonids, reapers, and other supernatural, preternatural, and mythological creatures she would love to find somewhere outside of her dreams is her greatest pleasure.

Her motto in life is simple, and it fuels her endless search into the

Otherworld: if anyone can imagine it, then it must exist somewhere.

Follow Roslyn at:

Universal Link: linktr.ee/roslynstclair

Website: https://roslynstclair.wixsite.com/my-site

Facebook: https://www.facebook.com/profile.php?id =100090441107257

Instagram: https://www.instagram.com/authorroslyn stclair/

OTHER BOOKS BY ROSLYN ST. CLAIR

Fated Archangels World (Either mentions or is in the world)

Softened- Fated Archangels, Lucifer's Prequel

https://books2read.com/u/47WjMq

Marked- Fated Archangels: Book One, Lucifer's Temptation

https://books2read.com/u/mpXyNX

Transcended- Fated Archangels: Book Two, Lucifer's Redemption

https://books2read.com/u/3k9nGW

*Clawed- A Fated Monsters Romance (by R. St. C) ...

https://books2read.com/u/mdqEAZ

To Marry A Succubus- A Monster Brides Romance ...

https://books2read.com/u/bQAqBZ

Fated to the Tarasque- A Monster Brides Romance ...

https://books2read.com/u/38YpAL

The Luckiest Vampire ... https://books2read.com/u/47vMKj

Lussi In Love– A Monster Brides Romance... https://books2read.com/u/mZlvre

A Special Krampus Kiss... https://books2read.com/u/me5vqY

Embracing My Guardian Demon – A Monster Brides Romance (release 2/15/25)

*Pain and Promises From the Monsters Under the Bed (R. St. C)... https://books2read.com/u/3y9V2l

*= Erotica

Other Worlds

The Vishap's Bride– A Monster Brides Romance ... https://books2read.com/u/bxBYPq

Want to discover more beastly brides and monstrous grooms? Keep reading the Monster Brides Romance Series!

Monster Brides Series Page
https://www.amazon.com/dp/B0C7TB9X1V

Haunted Hearts: A Monster Brides Romance
S.C. Principale
https://books2read.com/b/hauntedheartsmb

Ripples For Skies: A Monster Brides Romance
Teshelle Combs
https://books2read.com/ripplesforskiesmb

Betrothed to the Yeti: A Monster Brides Romance
Marilyn Barr
https://www.amazon.com/Betrothed-Yeti-Monster-Brides-Romance-ebook/dp/B0C7LNFF69/

As the Tide Turns: A Monster Brides Romance
Grace Mirchandani
https://a.co/d/6jxqCqd

The Vishap's Bride: A Monster Brides Romance
Roslyn St. Clair
https://books2read.com/u/bxBYPq

Claiming the Fae Crown: A Monster Brides
Romance

Lilliana Rose

books2read.com/u/3GpZ9L

A Wolf's Bargain

Rachel Abernathy

https://books2read.com/u/318eVn

Venom Kissed

Sydney Winward

https://books2read.com/u/mlpMWZ

To Marry A Succubus: A Monster Brides Romance
Roslyn St. Clair
https://books2read.com/u/bQAqBZ

Fated to the Tarasque
Roslyn St. Clair
https://books2read.com/u/b6G1k0

Phoenix's Eternal Flame

Sofia Aves

https://books2read.com/phoenixseternalflame

Nothing to Hyde

S.C. Principale

https://books2read.com/nothingtohyde

'Til Death Do Us Part…Or Not
Annee Jones
https://books2read.com/Til-Death-Do-Us-Part-Or-Not

In Love with the Leshy
Danielle Sibarium
https://books2read.com/b/b5YwL7

Marrying My MothLady

Marilyn Barr

https://www.amazon.com/gp/product/B0C7LR83QW

The Vampire's Mistress
D A Nelson
https://www.amazon.com/gp/product/B0CRS6W31C

Bite Me Tender, Bite Me Sweet
V.V. Strange
https://rb.gy/b83ned

Kraken's Vow

Raven Hush

https://books2read.com/krakensvow

His Undercover Wolf

Susan Horsnell

USA Today Bestselling Author

https://books2read.com/HisUndercoverWolf

Tide to the Selkie: A Monster Brides Romance
Serafina Jax
https://books2read.com/TidetotheSelkie

Hooking Captain Teeth
Marilyn Barr
https://www.amazon.com/gp/product/B0CLYKVC8
3

Stone Cold Groom
S.C. Principale
https://books2read.com/stonecoldgroom

Bonded to the Boo Hag: A Monster Brides
Romance
Mikayla Rand
https://books2read.com/BondedToTheBooHag

Kissing the Kelpie
Danielle Sibarium
https://books2read.com/u/4Xl2Kv

The Rusalka and Mr. Right
S.C. Principale
https://books2read.com/therusalkaandmrright

Bigfoot Finds A Bride: A Monster Brides Romance
Jenny Fenshaw
https://books2read.com/BigfootFindsABride

Frightfully Yours - A Tale of Love and
Nightmares
V.V. Strange
https://www.amazon.com/dp/B0DB9HHVH5

Lussi In Love: A Monster Brides Romance

Roslyn St. Clair
https://books2read.com/u/mZlvre

9 798227 600813